Book 1
THE NEW WORLD

Book 2
THE PARADOX

Book 3
THE MISSION

Preface

Attention, Attention: All Personnel prepare for dis-embarkment.

Peter Sullivan was never one to hit the ground running, and this moment was no exception. His eyes were blurry, stumbling, and confused; he wondered if he was dreaming.

The sleep shift was chaotic and confusing when the ship alarm system went off.

What's happening!? Everyone seemed to chant as they ran in a panic. Has anyone seen my wife? No time to question, one of the pilots yelled.

Peter kept asking the frantic crew as they ran by him, looking back at him as if he was crazy.

Was he?!!!! His family was aboard! Weren't they? As he ran down the smoke-filled corridor to the docking bay, he could hear the panic and desperate screaming, Abandon ship!!!! Quickly! Quickly!

Has anyone seen Lisa? Peter screamed as he quickly boarded the shuttle. The kids were kept somewhat of a secret from most of the crew. Peter squeezed his hands and prayed they were with their mother.

The Mission

Gary Robert Smith
Book III

The Mission
Copyright © 2024 by Gary Robert Smith

ISBN: 978-1639458981 (sc)
ISBN: 978-1639458998 (e)

All rights reserved. No part of this publication may be reproduced, distributed, or transmitted in any form or by any means, including photocopying, recording, or other electronic or mechanical methods, without the prior written permission of the publisher and/or the author, except in the case of brief quotations embodied in critical reviews and other noncommercial uses permitted by copyright law.

The views expressed in this book are solely those of the author and do not necessarily reflect the views of the publisher, and the publisher hereby disclaims any responsibility for them.

Writers' Branding
(877) 608-6550
www.writersbranding.com
media@writersbranding.com

Table of Contents

Preface ii
Dedication vii
Acknowledgment viii
From the Author ix
About the Author x
Chapter 1: *The Mission* *1*
Chapter 2: *The VIP's* *5*
Chapter 3: *Getting Ready to Fly* *12*
Chapter 4: *The Fortress* *18*
Chapter 5 *Boarding* *22*
Chapter 6 *Departure* *27*
Chapter 7: *Computer Forensic's* *32*
Chapter 8: *Set Adrift* *36*
Chapter 9 *Rehabilitation* *43*
Chapter 10: *Adaptation* *51*
Chapter 11: *A Seance* *58*
Chapter 12: *Meeting The God's* *63*
Chapter 13: *All the Kings Men* *71*
Chapter 14: *Nightmares* *78*
Chapter 15: *Captured* *81*
Chapter 16: *Your Majesty, Sir* *88*
Chapter 17: *No Casualties* *94*
Chapter 18: *A Grand Entrance* *100*
Chapter 19: *The Final Mission* *103*

Dedication

I dedicate this story to every Sci-Fi lover with an intimate passion for the power of the imagination and the resolution to accept plausible possibilities, however outlandish they may seem.
And to my children. My true Legacy

Acknowledgment

I want to thank the wonderful world of fiction.
Without it, we would indeed be lost.

From the Author

This story is written with the concept of plausibility coupled with the wonders of imagination. Fiction can help create the plausible if paired with the vision. Creativity has been the driving force for many of our cultural accomplishments today.

As a species, we constantly learn and long for the answers to the unknown. Science will test theories, and theories will challenge science.

Although theories and mythology are controversial and have produced dissenting opinions from Scientists and Clergymen alike, we celebrate their ideas.

To accept the wonders of the past, we must assume that ancient civilizations were a superior race.

We have always been perplexed by the enormous ruins and their meaning. The lack of tangible records doesn't explain what drove the ancients to such lunacy in needing to construct them. Time has all but erased any descriptions of the academic discipline that was required to accomplish their heritage. We are left with monumental structures and sparse objects of antiquity. Hieroglyphics can help decipher some of the past, but we can only speculate even with that.

Following the hypothesis that history repeats itself, we search for clues, hoping to find answers. Conveniently, thanks to science fiction, we can travel back in time and look for ourselves. With imagination and plausibility, we can see how it might have been so many years ago. It's all we have now.

So, let this sci-fi toil with your imagination, allow it to pair with plausibility, and see what you might find.

To quote the famous Serenity prayer, written by the great Theologian-philosopher Reinhold Niebuhr:

"*God grant me the serenity to accept the things we cannot change, the courage to change the things we can, and the wisdom to know the difference.*"

About the Author

Gary has always had a passion for writing, and being an avid Artist, Musician, and part-time critic has fueled that passion.

He has developed a unique writing style. His stories touch on science for a compelling perspective and still allow your imagination to lead the way.

Gary is a part-time musician who has followed his writing dream. Dabbling in songwriting, acting, and painting, his passion for science, and his love for realizable fiction, has brought forth this story. His good characters are warm, loving, and easy going. His bad guys? Not so much.

His life's knowledge stems from diverse work experiences. From blue collar to blue jeans, he has seen life through the Windshield of a long-haul truck, at the wheel of a warehouse forklift, behind the lens of a portrait camera, and operating a computer design software, all while delving into the beautiful world of fiction.

Honing and perfecting his writing since early 1980, he has engaged his audiences, giving them the power of imagination, mating the plausible with the possible. Thanks to the universal love for fiction, he brings you The Mission.

Chapter 1

THE MISSION

During the days of space exploration, almost everyone on the Planet Poseidon was equipped with a backyard makeshift telescope, monitoring the night-lit skies in hopes of discovering a new home. At least ten planets were considered each week. According to the astrophysicists, a winning planet had to be carbon-based with a tempered atmosphere. A mixture of oxygen, hydrogen, and Carbon Dioxide was the key. Scientists and astronomers alike were eager to get involved. Once the promising Planet was finally identified, the Major Space The agency kicked into action, but the gossip quickly circulated. Narratives seemed to come out from everywhere. Everyone was suddenly an expert in the field of space travel.

Religious preachers boasted, "We now can explore other worlds like our own and be able to see God's work in its entirety." GC (Grand Central) published in its daily journal (The GC Inquire) in an unsuccessful attempt to weaken enthusiasm since the public interest quickly outgrew its production capabilities. The article read; The Mission to a New World could prove to be challenging," and volunteers should be robust in their convictions. The column went on to explain the dangers of uncharted space travel. The tiny print at the bottom of the advertisement stated that there was a possibility of a one-way trip for the first responders. The road to the new world was new, and GC could not predict its tribulations.

(GC) was the primary manufacturer of retrofit parts for spacecraft and low-orbit vessels and, consequently, employed most of the surrounding townspeople in its many production departments. The company offered four-year college programs tailored to fit GC's criteria. Upon graduation, a student became eligible for on-the-job pilot training. Everyone knew shuttles would eventually be valuable during a prolonged space flight. A closer look at a potential surface would be ideal for determining the livability, although the smaller ships did not possess high-tech equipment. Probes were meant to test atmospheric conditions. The deciding probe was a little floating ball-shaped object the size of a gaming sphere, approximately 12 meters in diameter.

Until recently, the shuttles were used to load and unload passengers, their luggage, and supplies for the large vacation ships anchored above the Planet's Gavity. It seemed the high technology of space flight offered an exciting adventure for the rich and was enjoyed by many who could afford it. However, with the new Planet Discovery, GC would have to delay the sought-after luxury service.

The new project was named The Mission and was in full swing as hopefuls reserved their spots. Each shuttle was capable of transporting forty-nine crew members. Fifty counting the pilot, and with that many lives in their hands, they had to be accomplished flyers. The pilot training was stringent, forcing some to drop out halfway through, but it didn't exclude them from the project. All GC's graduates were granted passage to the Fortress as long as they passed the physical. The crew affectionately called the shuttles "little lifeboats."

These pioneering travelers' dreams and aspirations had finally become a reality, putting aside all doubts and skepticism from the old-school thinkers. Investments came in the hopes of a lucrative return. Grand Central heavily invested in the development of the Vessel. This flying Fortress had waited on GC's back burner for years. The ship would be their claim to fame, and the invention of the (EAHPE), "Extreme Accelerated Hypersonic Power Engine," made it exulting. The speed and efficiency of the unit were unquestionably supreme. They installed the smaller Hyper engines in some of the shuttles and gave senior pilots picking rights, although they often chose the older original crafts out of familiarity and comfort. The Fortress would employ sixteen retrofitted shuttles within their fleet.

******

Amateurs and some professional astronomers argued about who made the first sighting, which created disgruntled communities. They even staged a rally in the streets with picket signs claiming the spotlight was misguided, chanting they were being unfair to the real heroes. Signs read (GIVE CREDIT WHERE CREDIT IS DUE)

Instead of new possibilities, hopes, and dreams, they conjured hostilities and fearful doubts. Rumors started circulating about their own failing Planet and how it was doomed for destruction. War and famine had taken away most of its resources. The longer they spread the narratives, the sooner the demise became. The outlining communities asked,

"Why else would the astronomers be looking for new planets if they weren't genuinely buying into the well-known propaganda of the "END OF THE WORLD, prediction."

More and more people started believing the rumors of a dying Planet. Some loyalists still felt the Planet was salvageable and ignored the lecturer's persistence, attempting to counter the narratives. They formed small battalions at first, with dedicated supporters to push back. GC wasn't guaranteeing an oasis within the Mission project, just an alternative solution. For the travelers who chose to leave, the idea of it being better than what they had on Poseidon was enough. It wouldn't have mattered to most inhabitants since the current situation around them was blatantly obvious. Most were tired of constantly looking over their shoulder for fear of a disgruntled soldier looking to recruit or destroy them.

Fanatics were stockpiling supplies. Others started categorizing priority levels for the waiting list, saying, "GC was only interested in the capital generated above the cost." The talk was that your annual income would dictate your ride off the Planet, and the poor would die with it. This irrational thought brought phobia and discontent. In reality, the trip was not a large purchase. GC considered it a small investment in their new life with a promise to work for the betterment of the new populous. Significant capital for the Mission came from donations and taxes, which GC returned to the project. High- dollar investors were given contracts stating conditions that would bring them perks and exemptions on any new business endeavors. It wasn't enough for the successful entrepreneur to escape a stagnant planet; they wanted to ensure they maintained their significance.

Still, Planet Poesidon's ruling was not far behind them, and the law and order of the new Planet would eventually catch up to the travelers after they settled. For most passengers, escaping and starting a new life was a blessing, given the option of re-inventing themselves. They knew it was troubling times, and hoping for a New World in the balance was a welcoming relief. With the Cliché,

"What would euphoria be without its sister doom." They kept the momentum of the program going.

However, the public that maliciously spread the negative rumors was partially correct. Their home planet had supported life for billions of years but was currently in depletion. It had been known by most planetary scholars for years. Predictions of overpopulation and complacency were being blamed. As a result, space travel was getting massive amounts of attention.

The founder of GC, Robert Sinclair, was following his dream and, consequently, his reason for the Mission. He felt he knew more than what was being told. In his mind, the species was at the end of its life cycle, and he hated the idea of doing nothing to prevent it. Robert wanted to save his species from extinction. There was plenty of proof of it existing already. Fossils and buried bones show a completely different life in the past. He saw the end coming long before it became rumored. Initially, he wanted to go with the first ship out but decided to wait until the new Planet's foundation was in place. "At least a village, at best a town." He would say, "I'm not much for having to rough it at my age. I'd only be in the way." He would exclaim.

The Mission was the savior and extension of the Posiedon civilizations. Unbeknownst to the general public, not everyone would be allowed into the Mission project. A rebellious movement was taking place over the country, creating civil unrest, and was considered by some to be the reason for the evaluation. A new start was how GC saw it, and they did not want the rebellions involved. The advertisements never mentioned any special considerations. They kept the operation's objective a secret, believing that, for the Mission to succeed, the participants had to be hand-picked, and broadcasting that would worsen matters. Robert felt that the Mission was not meant to save the Planet, but an attempt at starting over with a clean slate, with a new breed of people.

Chapter 2

THE VIP'S

Peter Sullivan couldn't sleep. The clock read 1:20 a.m. Twenty minutes later than the last time he looked. His early morning appointment with Doctor Miller was the first step in granting passage to Mission I. It was going to be a busy day, he thought. Grand Central had Peter scheduled for the entire day, with required vaccines, a health analyst, briefings, interviews, and mockup familiarity. Peter had waited so long for this day that he bubbled with excitement, and his thoughts raced.

Had he convinced his wife of twenty-five years to trust him? This was the chance to carry on the bloodline of humanity. Peter had never been the kind to follow. His leadership qualities earned him respect and integrity throughout his career at the College. He was the head of the Astronomy Department at Fillmore University, and had the privilege of using the Big Telescope located in the on-campus observatory. It was so big that it had to be operated with hydraulics just to turn it for tracking. Housed inside a dome, it could isolate portions of the night sky for an in-depth study. Needless to say, Peter loved his job. Much taller than his colleagues, he automatically gained respect from any student he associated with. Holding his youth, he always wore a plaid sports coat and casual running shoes and was often mistaken for a student. At the first encounter, his dark brown eyes left one with mixed perceptions, Although his honesty and open-book personality quickly changed that prespective. With dark hair and olive skin, all the female admirers called him "eye candy." When the opportunity for New Planet council became available, he couldn't turn it down.

******

As Professor Sulivan entered the Hospital doors, his anxiety was overpowering.

The People's Hospital was built around what used to be a military medical unit.

The area had since grown into a busy metropolis with an enormous power plant that supported most of the city's population and gave electricity to the surrounding areas. The township was well known for its Churches. They were abundant for anyone needing guidance. It was rumored that the crime rate was low in the area, so it brought in many peace seekers, sometimes resulting in political conversations among long-time locals. New school versed Old school.

Most people had good intentions, but others sometimes didn't agree with the general method, others used to keep the peace. "It was an ongoing struggle," Doctor Jason Miller would say. He tried to avoid the area's politics, but being a sympathizer made it hard to turn away.

The talk had died down in winter months as most people frequenting the public establishments, avoided the frigid weather.

The Doctor cursed as he strenuously turned the frozen lock to the laboratory entrance. "Why am I the only one they trust to open this antique excuse for an office?" but the Doctor was usually anything but cranky around his colleagues. All his associates loved and respected him and were often said to be always willing to help. This winter had been an icy one. The cold on his hairless head increased his frustration, since he left his hat home.

"It's always on the electric vehicle," he cursed. Spending most of his time in biological study, he recently turned his focus to fatal diseases of the nervous system and the breakdown of Pyron Proteins. The Doctor had lost his wife to Kuru eight years back and preferred his studies over the city's conflicts nowadays. As it turned out, the Pryon Proteins were the leading cause of Kuru. A debilitating disease that attacks the nervous system, causing paralyzation of all internal organs. His efforts earned him an Academic Award in the field of his research. Unfortunately, his research came too late to save

The Mission

his loved one. Being the first to discover the condition gave him the honor of naming it although the devastation it inflicted, was nothing he cared to honor. He called it Kuru after his dog. (Little Kuru), had died very quickly two years earlier for no apparent reason at the time. The peculiarity of it seemed all too familiar once his wife went down with it. They exhibited glossy eyes and exhaustion. Little Kuru barely got up long enough to eat. It was tough to once again, witness his wife's struggle.

With no personal ties to the community other than his upstanding status, Jason quickly accepted the medical officer position when offered since he was eager for a change. Giving his knowledge to a handful of patients on a pre-destined ship was not a prestigious title, but then again, titles no longer interested him. He had no desire to stay on a dying planet with no predicted future. Jason had always regarded himself as a ground-breaking pioneer anyway. He was offered a chance to start over with his career, which, in his Twenty-five years of practice in the only medical unit he'd ever known, was beginning to weigh on him. He relished the idea of a change.

******

Grand Central had devised the plan to save humanity for those resourceful Types. They were told it wouldn't be easy, but the alternative of staying on the current Planet that would not support their grandchildren's children was a convincing reality. Jason had nothing to lose but a chance to restart his life and his future on a new horizon. You'll always have doomsday slayers. "GC knew what they were doing." He thought. They produced quality work for years and were a trusted company. He was convinced it would be a safe and secure Mission.

The Doctor always started his day early. His comrades would say Jason doesn't work to live. He lives to work, which he never denied.

******

"Good Morning, Jason. How are you today?" His assistant, Sarah Clark, commented as she entered the Office.

"Good morning," he replied. "Is it nine o'clock already?"

"No, it's only 8:30. I thought I'd start early this morning."

"Excellent, Jason exclaimed. We have an extensive roster to fill today.

It seems everyone wants to go into space." he commented without looking up, buried in his ledger.

"Can you get Bill Strauss on the phone for me? "Now, where did I leave my recorder?" he thought out loud.

******

Professor William Strass was on his way to his top-floor Office. His prestigious level currently gave him the title of senior Biologist at the University. He disliked the daily monotonous elevator climb, although his experimental cultures seemed to survive better at the higher altitude.

He was pleasantly surprised to hear Sarah Clark's voice on the line.

They had attempted a relationship with each other in College without success, they had mutually agreed to be friends. The compatibility was excellent, but the chemistry was lacking. Bill seemed to have a roaming eye when he was younger, which kept him a bachelor for most of his life. "Just can't find the right woman." He'd proclaim. William was a handsome, blond-haired, medium-build, all-around jock type. He always participated in all his school's sports teams. Team spirit was his motto. He was agile and competent enough to come out on top when scoring for the team. The coach called him a natural. The school's support group would always refer to him as the old silver-tongued Bill. Despite his pragmatic love life, he still had a way with the ladies.

It was no surprise that GC would be contacting him. He was a brilliant, almost famous man.

******

"Hello, Bill, this is Sarah Clark."

I'd know that sweet voice anywhere. How are you? Bill quickly replied.

"Good, considering."

"Sarah, I'm still pining for you, sweetheart. What have you been doing with yourself lately?"

"Keeping busy, Bill. We should get together, sometime soon. I could bring you up to date."

"Is it a Dinner Date, then?" He said, "So, tell me, what can I do for you?"

"Well, I'm working for Jason Miller now, and he….."

"WHAT! That old workhorse!?" Bill exclaimed.

"He's not that bad. He wants to speak with you. I'll transfer you. We can talk later."

She chuckled at his pining comment as she pushed the appropriate buttons to make the switch." He always was an old smoothie, she thought. He had the most beautiful blue eyes. I wonder if he still likes sailing."

******

If anyone were to ask to explain Sarah Clark, they would say, "pleasant, efficient, helpful, and amazingly crafty. She had an uncanny ability to see things that others didn't. She was nicknamed Clairvoyant Sarah by many of her friends.

******

"Good morning. I'm here for my appointment." Peter excitedly said as he gazed at the beautiful woman, suddenly noticing his unconscious stare.

"Mr. Sullivan, I believe," she said, checking the schedule. "Peter, is it?"

"Yes,, Sorry, I forgot my own name for a minute."

"Didn't sleep last night huh?

"Barley"

"You can call me Sarah…. Have you finished filling out the forms?" She asked with a slight smile on her lips.

"No, not yet."

"Not to worry, you can finish it at home."

She replied, handing him "The novel," as Peter called it, for its book-like appearance.

Just then, the Doctor peeked around the corner.

"Professor Sullivan?" He asked as he leaned over the counter, "Are you ready for some tests?"

"That's why I'm here, Doctor."

"Good, Sarah!" Dr. Strauss will call me back with the results of some cultures I left with him last week. Let me know, will you? It's essential."

"Will do, Doctor."

"Have you had the Kuru vaccination yet?" Sarah could hear them fading away as the two walked down the hall.

Gary Robert Smith

******

It was 2:00 (afternoon) when Peter left the Doctor's Office and headed home. Peter's wife kept herself rather busy during her husband's preparation time. It helped keep her mind off the idea of possibly never seeing Peter again.

When Peter arrived home later that day, the house was empty. There was a message on the recorder flashing.

Hi, honey, I'm with Judy. I'll be at the Museum today. They have a new display of ancient social cultures of prehistoric cultures. I hope they have done their research correctly with the current studies on the subject. I like what I'm hearing about it, and I think I can refer to some of their findings in my book.

Lisa Sullivan was considered a novice writer within the community and had published one book on Ancestral Influence on Contemporary culture the year before. Sales increased after the recent discovery. Many readers believed in diverse cultures and liked relating them to the possibility of other planets and understanding them with them should it become necessary.

Peter started to feel his sleepless nights and thought it best to nap before the kids got home. It was the late afternoon of day five. Four days left until departure.

******

Honey? Are you home? Lisa quietly peeked in the bedroom door to see Peter sleeping.

Lisa Sullivan was a beautifully intelligent young woman. She had very long dark hair, which she always wore up. Her cute little glasses that seemed to frame her round face helped grant her respect and acceptance in the community. With a business major, she was very resourceful in many ways and stubborn in many others. Especially when it came to her husband, she knew that Peter was struggling with the child restrictions as much as she was. It was anticipated to be a four-year turnaround back to Poseidon to reload each time until the roster was complete. Children in their last year of scholarship had to finish the curriculum before leaving. This was not for another year for the Sullivans, and GC was unwilling to delay the project just for a few families.

This was so biased and unfair to Lisa. She planned to intervene and challenge the decisions of the agency. Her research had helped her to a point,

The Mission

but her scenarios weren't panning out. She also knew that chances needed to be taken. She told no one of her investigations and was willing to accept the outcome of her actions, which had to be kept confidential. "There was too much invested in her marriage for anyone to question her motives." She thought.

Still, the consequence wouldn't have mattered. Lisa was a determined young lady. As she jotted down notes in her notebook, Peter entered the room.

"Hi honey, have you eaten dinner yet?" She asked.

Rubbing his eyes as he tried to focus on the wall clock.

"Where's the kids?"

"Bobby called. She's spending the night at Carol's."

"Jim is at Ball practice."

"If you're hungry, I can throw something together for you."

"That's okay. I'll make a Targee. I still have some forms to fill out."

With the Mission being in uncharted space. There were unspoken dangers that Peter kept from his family.

The possibility of it being a one-way trip impeded his conscience, although Lisa was never one to be left in the dark. She was a resourceful young professional. Peter knew she was aware, but he didn't want to stress it and possibly conjure more doubt. He needed things to be positive. Above all, the children needed to stay positive.

They all understood the profession their father had chosen sometimes took him away from the family. Sometimes out of the country for months, but never for years, and certainly not five years. He explained to them how he would be one of the pioneers who helped relocate to the New World and that it was a good thing. To go down in history as a hero. They should be proud of being part of the movement. The word, MARTER, never entered the conversation, although FAMOUS did.

Chapter 3

GETTING READY TO FLY

(GC) Grand Central's agency headquarters made their home on the 50th floor of a building that stood atop a manufactured mountain.

The rubbles of a burned city of the ancient past had been piled and stacked in a four-kilometer square area. The building stood strong enough to withstand extreme weather patterns and active geometric disasters. It housed the hagiarchy of all dominions, including the head of state.

As Captain Paul Zeiger rode the elevator up, he could feel the pressure increasing in his ears. The decor of the building reminded him of the career successes he had achieved in his life. Copies of life honor awards of many foot soldiers hung on the courtyard walls with hundreds of plaques to remember the fallen. A life to which many had the privilege of donating.

It was the city's pulse. Small amounts of oxygen had to be circulated to the top five floors through the venting system to keep the tenants alert.

A "GC Permission pass" was required above floors forty-five. The pass was obtained through a quick application, but it required a personal background check, which could sometimes take weeks to receive. The company knew that with the uprising around the country, too many disagreed with the company's evac ideas. GC took all precautions for safety.

The VIP elevators were guarded by security personnel at the door. They would automatically skip the first forty-five floors, rocketing the riders to forty-six and above. The option of stopping on the 46th floor to adjust to the atmospheric pressure was another fringe benefit the building offered VIP's.

The Mission

There was a breakfast bar to relax in while adjusting. Upon returning to the ground, the elevator would reset itself for a reload. The guards assured all passengers were cardholders, but the real protector was a fingerprint scan just outside the rotating gates. GC wasn't taking any chances of a security breach.

******

The first spring day was beautiful as Paul Zeager taxied to the launchpad. He appeared much younger than his exclaimed years with slightly greying hair and chiseled looks. He prided himself on keeping fit.

The thought of retirement was far from his mind. Paul had delved into his passion years before the significant cosmic discovery.

He had always been a societal leader and a willing recipient of responsibility. After attending the state's high-level university of education, he applied for GC's pilot training as an instructor.

Initially, he started in Astronomy but switched to Propulsion Dynamics after his first year. GC favored all prestigious University students. Paul was an accomplished pilot throughout school, having built his hover plane and mountain jumper as a kid, breaking a few records. GC was impressed with Paul's commitment to his passion, although his slight recklessness was a concern.

"One needs to take chances in life," was his opinion. "If I crash and die, it was meant to be. My Karma hasn't caught up to me yet."

His accomplishments in service was impressive, bringing GC to the unanimous decision and final nomination for Captain of the Mission. There were no others of his caliber available. Paul was a shoo-in.

He was named "King of the Air" while serving in the military. He had spent his entire service with a spotless record.

Paul was grateful for all his praise. "It's what I do," he'd say. "You do your thing. I'll do mine. But commit to it, and you will succeed."

******

The first shuttle was packed with supplies and lifted off without a glitch. Docking with the Fortress got a little tricky, though. It seems the alignment system was slightly off-caliber. Seems the memory lock was shorting out, forcing them to adjust it manually each time upon arrival.

"Better get that fixed before departure." The Captain commented.

Raymond Taylor was seated at the Navagater's chair, checking the itinerary. He slid over to the commlink and hit the button to contact his friend in receiving.

Lenard stood at the loading dock, accepting the delivery of miscellaneous items.

"Lenny, come in," his comm-link buzzed.

"Whatcha need, Ray?"

"Have you gotten any uniforms in?"

"Yeah, want to come to get yours?"

"If you don't mind, I'm tired of my civvies. They remind me of the old place, and I'm so ready to move on."

"Sure, come on down."

Raymond was a man of short stature but not of character. His size was such that his clothes would have to be custom-made to fit. He was an honest, good man. He always came through in times of trouble, especially to his friends, and gave respect to all he came in contact with.

Having a carefree disposition, he always made light if he felt a conversion was starting to turn solum. During crew meetings, Ray sometimes said odd things and smiled to see what kind of reaction he'd get. Not that he loved controversy, just a little harmless sarcasm was sometimes needed to calm an intense conversation.

Ray and Lenny had been good friends all through childhood. They'd been lucky enough to accompany each other on most all space flights, attributing to the fact that Paul Zeager liked them both. Lenny swore he'd never volunteer for any ship unless Paul were on it. Unfortunately, it didn't always work out that way. GC wasn't in the habit of asking for volunteers within the operations department. GC, however, did know the ones that worked well together.

******

Shuttles stayed busy all week, non-stop. They ran shifts to complete the task. A few pilots felt the sooner they got off this Planet, the better. The upper echelon was the first to board for preparation requirements. Some came on a supply run, others got the more congenial treatment. Paul Zeager preferred the loaded supply shuttle to avoid the commotion.

The Mission

A supply run was a bit shaky at first. It was heavy off the start but much smoother after escaping the gravitational pull.

It was a buzzing of activity that day. As the Captain entered the Bridge, he grabbed a copy of the crew roster.

Taking his place at the helm, he noticed Ray sitting at the control monitor.

"Let's see who I have to work with here." The Captain said. He combed over the list as he sat in his custom-made chair. "Who is this, Sarah Clark?" He insisted.

"Don't know. You'll have to ask headquarters," Raymond replied. "I think she works for the Doctor. Maybe his assistant?"

"Assistant!" The Captain snapped, "Since when does Jason Miller need an assistant? Sorry Ray, Don't answer that." He said with a smile.

"Maybe she's administrative help?" Ray shrugged.

******

The Captain and Doctor Miller knew each other through their service in the military. Paul flew the wounded into the Miller's mobile hospital. Sometimes alive, sometimes dead. Whether they would make it in time to save the injured soldier's lives was a gamble. The military experience left a scar on everyone's heart. It would automatically bond the ones who shared in the trauma.

"It's not what we didn't do. It's what we did do that matters." Paul would tell it.

"Our recovery rate of the fatally wounded was over half." They had both dealt with death enough times but never grew resistant to the despair it left within.

A war would do that to so many men. With that shared experience, they stayed in touch long afterward. Remembering the times of younger days rather than the good old days. Paul remembered. *"There were more accomplishments than there were failures.'*

******

"Looks like GC had chosen the best this time out." He thought, combing the roster. Paul had flown on many excursions in his career and seen many ships, but this ship took the trophy! He thought.

15

The ship housed shuttles. Mainly needed at their destination to transport personnel back to ground level. A shuttle and a good pilot were invaluable to the Mission—pilot training expertise, ship maneuverability, and accurate firepower were vital for their welfare. The Astronomic Academy of Pilots (AAP) had nearly removed the Space Piracy of the past, but there was still that looming potential. Looting would happen periodically, especially if a flight was thought to be carrying valuables.

******

The city's local law enforcement was kept busy with the disgruntled rebellers. The Planet was going through a hectic re-establishment of leaders. The detention houses were at their maximum. What they couldn't confine, they were forced to give release deeds to the lesser offenders, with the option of turning a new lifestyle through tax-paid programs. Many of the higher-level desperate criminals were flown to a deserted Island, far removed from civilization or any space relocation program, to help prevent any illegal stowaways.

Civil unrest was prominent with stubborn opinions. There didn't seem to be a good solution, and many conversations resulted in physical confrontations. Either side claimed the other side was lying about their convictions. Accusations went around and around until injuries and sometimes death resulted.

GC had previously established a shuttle airfield in the country, away from the commotion of the city. The field owner and farmer of the land gladly donated the plot for their use in return for a seat on the first shuttle. His request was quickly accepted since his farming skills would be necessary in the new world. Masons with construction skills were welcomed, and many had already accepted their offer.

The medical professionals were given the finer rooms on the ship since GC was grateful they were willing to leave their lucrative practices behind, especially during bloody wartime. Still, government control was slipping, and the economy suffered severely. Most patients could not pay for their medical services, and Doctors, having taken an oath to protect and save, couldn't turn them away. Drugs that only prolonged a terminal disease were not proscribed

The Mission

due to the cost, so the ill slowly passed, usually suffering. Moving on was a comforting alternative compared to the chaotic system one would leave behind.

******

When leaving town, a land vehicle would take approximately half a Poseidon hour to reach the loading area. It wasn't a covert operation, but the open field provided the space needed for the shuttles. Supplies were delivered by land vehicles and staged for loading, allowing the pilots to work nonstop. The warehouse in the city's heart stored non-perishable goods for the Mission. Wrapping and packaging occurred constantly, day and night, in preparation. Five cargo vehicles left the warehouse completely loaded and were driven to the staging field to be delivered to the Fortress. All the volunteers who helped unload the trucks were also promised a seat on the first run.

It was no easy task preparing a ship of this size. The momentum of the launch was growing with excitement. *Are we ready to fly yet?* was the on-board buzz of shipmates.

Chapter 4

THE FORTRESS

The Fortress was a castle in the sky. Its enormous size and streamlined shape left shuttle passengers in awe as they approached boarding. It was called "The Mission," named after the project. It housed GC's forty-five shuttles, their respective pilots, and its thousand crew members at its maximum.

Some shuttle pilots were young and fresh to deep space travel, but all had logged the required hours for emergency operations. They were very comfortable and efficient little vehicles. They had a payload of fifty passengers each. With the first trip skeleton crew, they would use only half of the available ships for loading. Each shuttle came equipped with winching capabilities for towing disabled crafts. That information was kept on the low down so as not to frighten the travelers with any ideas of a possible disabled ship. Still, the agency affirmed safety. Backup systems were built into all ship designs.

******

Shuttle pilots were taught to respect their craft, but some of the younger ones, with empty cargo, would often fly trick maneuvers on the way back down to break the monotony. It was all fun and games until one pilot crashed to the ground, obliterating the ship and killing himself. As to who the trickster was, there wasn't much of him left to identify aside from the process of elimination within the roster for that given day. He was a young rogue with a history of disobeying authority.

They attributed it to vertiginous after examining the circumstances. The report said, "Due to his flying ability, he got too close to the ground during an unorthodox landing." A clause was later written in the employment agreement stating, "No pilot maneuvers or otherwise routines outside of GC's safety standards were to be initiated by any pilot regardless of their experience. Punishable by removal of all rights given to them by GC." The pilots were all grounded until they signed it, pushing the departure set date back a few days and gradually returning on duty. GC did an interview inquiry with all pilots before they were put back into service. Background checks became mandatory. The older ones were already in the system, but the rookies needed to be checked back into their civilian days. It was something GC should have done beforehand, but with the excitement of the new discovery, it somehow got overlooked. The success of any Mission depends on the honesty and transparency of all involved.

Chatter started circulating in town, commenting, "Sure hope this isn't an omen of Mission failure."

The cargo bay was filling quickly to compensate for the lost time. Instead of double duty, which could cause even more injuries, they decided to use larger containers for packing, designed to stack much more uniformly. More supplies with fewer trips was a stellar idea.

GC's Chief Executive Officer commended himself. The larger container didn't matter on the ship since stacking was easy in zero gravity. The Fortress was the first ship to have been built in zero gravity. It was quite an exciting process to watch, the Captain thought. In his entire career, he had never been this well- equipped. GC thought of everything. This ship is much bigger than the last one. It was so well-engineered. It is so well planned, with an estimated life span of four generations.

The ship was built so well that it was said to be a homestead for those who chose not to pilgrimage to another planet. Once the word got out, volunteers lined up for the waiting list. The talk was, "With Fortress living, you'd know what to expect." Not everyone was the pioneering type, and that circulating narrative was GC's convincing factor in starting the construction initially. Before moving in, the homesteaders would have to wait until the massive movement diminished.

Gary Robert Smith

******

GC denied the ship's existence for years but couldn't deny the interest. The project had been in place since the upheaval and discontent of the Planet, but it was kept under scrutiny due to the overwhelming widespread interest that GC knew they weren't prepared for. A second Fortress would be built should this migration get extreme. With the demand for homesteaders, a second ship was needed. GC was amazed at how many applied for homesteading.

The Fortress was built in the secret weightlessness of space. Still, with all the rumors flying around at home, the secret didn't last long. It was such a big ship that eventually, during its construction, it could be seen using the most crude homemade telescopes from the home planet. The Ship's Artificial gravity was the latest addition, supplied by Graveforce. A scholar scientist within Graveforce discovered that force depended on mass and movement. Centrifugal force was the answer, which relied on passenger's movement throughout the ship.

Unfortunately, resistance played a crucial role in the formula's consistency. Even though it was the keystone to prolonged space travel. Having gone through several iterations, it was less than perfect.

It would change due to fluctuating rotational Speeds. Nothing substantial, but noticeable. The rotation was affected by the mass it supported. The balance would alter the rotation if too many passengers assembled in a specific area. It wasn't a big problem for the first pioneers since they were a lesser crew, but it could be an area of concern once they started transporting the remainder of the Planet.

Passengers were all alerted of this problem through the book forms Saraha Clark initially allocated during ship commencement. The Fortress was designed to disperse passenger weight by giving them alternate routes to their destinations. For instance, several entrances to the café came from different areas of the ship. A schedule was set up for food service as not to overload the restaurant.

It worked to their advantage during loading and stacking supplies. The lighter gravity could be manually adjusted, enabling longer work hours with less fatigue. For that reason, the loading dock was operated independently from the crew.

The engineering crew had the daily task of adjusting the gravity, like tuning a musical instrument. It was a minor inconvenience compared to the unhealthy weightlessness affecting the health of a body. Thanks to Graveforce, Muscle and bone deterioration was eliminated. The Fortress was cutting-edge technology. It was said to have all the comforts of home.

The ship was so large that it encompassed a tri-level layout. The town level was the entire first level. It housed Stores, entertainment facilities, personal offices, Doctor's offices, and a mini hospital. Enlisted crew on 2nd level, Officers on 3rd. The top floor was round, giving the Captain a 360-open view of the bridge sitting on a swivel throne.

The ship's tail, which appeared from a distance like a bubble about to explode. It housed the agriculture department and would maintain and replenish the plants and animals for the trip, eventually helping cultivate the new Planet.

Grand Central also made a mockup bridge of the vessel for home engineering reference during the Mission. They expected to have complete radio contact and kept an ongoing, three-shift working force to accommodate. It was also used as a training model to offer a hands-on understanding of ship operations.

The Top officers were brought to the Fortress ahead of their support crew to prepare the computers and set up the intelligence for planet communications. They were also meant to establish themselves in the slightly intimidating environment of flashing lights, mini-monitors, and one big screen encompassing the 360-degree area. Mockup was a start, but working on-site gave them a better feel for the ship.

The Fortress was elaborate for a good reason. If cultivating was not accessible on the new Planet, a comfortable ship environment was essential, if only for morals. If the new Planet was favorable, the Fortress would return for an entire crew to start the second migration. Captain Zeager was slated to make the initial trip only before becoming a passenger back to the new Planet or homesteader on the ship. A new Captain would take it from that point.

Chapter 5

Boarding

With departure pre-scheduled, Peter was packing personal hygiene and what little leisure clothes he was permitted. He thought, "*This was it.*" he threw the bag over his shoulder and headed down to the kitchen where Lisa was preparing breakfast while talking to her com link.

"Okay, good," she said to the other line as Peter entered the room.

"Thank you so much. You've been a Godsend," she said as she quickly pushed the button to disconnect.

"It got a little scary towards the end, referring to my roster pick," Peter said as he stepped into the kitchen.

"Honey, I knew you'd make it onboard."

"Are you coming for the launch?"

Lisa paused momentarily, then replied without turning around to face him.

"You know how I hate Goodbye. You better hurry. Isn't this the last shuttle to the ship?"

"It's mock-up familiarization today. My shuttle leaves early in the morning. I'll be spending tonight in the mock-up."

Although Peter was pleased to see Lisa more at ease, he was slightly confused by her sudden attitude change. He half expected her to at least show some emotion before he left. She seemed almost cold.

"Kids! Take care of your mother. I love you all. I'll call you before I leave."

"You'd better!!!" The kids yelled in unison.

The Mission

Peter said, "See you in six years," with a half-smile on his lips.

The round trip was calculated to be four years. Two years out, two years back, and another two years for the second load. Six years would have passed before the family reunited. That was if everything went as planned. Once the new home was established, GC would send ships back to back. The kids, being that much older and considered young adults by then, would be given the option of staying, which Lisa had to consider. To Lisa, it was almost like GC intentionally tried to destroy the family through unfair policies. She thought she knew Peter well enough to know he wouldn't be doing this to be a Marter. He had too much compassion for the family unit.

As Peter entered the land transport en route to the mock-up, he wondered what caused the change in his wife's attitude. She's always been a little anxious about the Mission. She dreaded it and even cried some nights when she thought Peter was already asleep. He knew how much she was hurting, but he was confident that Mission Control was correct in its calculations. It would be a safe, secure mission, and the ship would return to Posieden in four years.

******

"Permission to come aboard, Sir," echoed through the loading dock as each shuttle emptied passengers.

The next day was no less busy loading high-ranking personnel. The Captain stood reluctantly at the shuttle landing pad. Ten shuttles were in a staggered sequence, bringing up personnel.

"Permission to come aboard, Sir." was ringing in Zieger's ear.

"Your name?" He added, and each one quickly responded.

"Permission granted," the Captain replied, never looking up from his roster.

As the ship slowly loaded, Zeager got impatient. "*I have much more pressing issues to attend besides admissions.*" He frustratingly thought. "*The programs for the ship needed to be loaded. The intercom for all the stations away from the bridge needed to be confirmed. Logs needed to be set up and inserted into the online system*".

He knew Lenny would have taken care of it already, but it all needed to be confirmed and signed off before launch. If there was a problem with anything, it could delay the start, and Paul liked staying on top of things.

A sweet little voice broke Paul's concertation.

Paul looked at the roster. "So you're Sarah Clark?"

"Yes, Sir. I'll be loading the rest of the crew once the GC officers are all on board."

"Oh, please relieve me, all Officers are on board. The door is your's." Zeager said and hurried away.

Peter was relieved to see Sarah.

"Hello, Miss Clark, permission to come aboard."

"Professor Sulivan, how are you?"

"A little shaken from the shuttle ride up; other than that, fine."

"Yes, that sometimes happens. I don't mean to add insult to injury, but I don't see you on the list. Let me contact GC. Wait by the side."

She motioned for Raymond to take over and, minutes later, came back with a spare room and an apology from headquarters.

"A slight overlook, I'm sure, Mr Sullivan. So sorry."

******

Finding his room was easy enough. GC had designed the crew's lodging floors identically, except the officer's doors were marked with a nameplate. Peter wasn't concerned that his door plate was blank. After the identity confusion at Bording, he was just glad he was here.

"An Omen? he thought. *"After all the hoops GC had put him through, then to end up in a vacant room 313?"* Fortunately, he was not a superstitious man.

His thoughts raced with the adventure ahead, the empty house he had left Lisa with, and his trust in the agency's abilities to safely deliver his family to their new home. Peter had experienced anxiety before, but this had to be the worst.

Doctor Miller had anticipated it and supplied all passengers with medication. Slowly unpacking what little supplies he was allowed to bring, his nerves calmed. He was tired from the boarding regiment and the stress of leaving his family behind. The adrenaline was letting him go, and wanting to rest, he preferred little or no talk. As he lay across the bed, what seemed to be minutes later, the room buzzer went off. He saw a young lad in his twenties, dressed in civic's, standing in the hall through the viewport. *What could this youngster want?* He thought. Peter flipped the intercom switch.

"Yes?"

"Mr. Sullivan?" The lad asked.

The Mission

"Yes, again."

"The Captain requests a casual present tonight in the Round Room after the evening meal."

"Okay, thank you."

******

The round room had multiple uses. Originally meant as a conference room, this time used to meet, mingle, and help familiarize all passengers. It could also serve as a celebration room if needed. With its spherical shape, the acoustics produced a softer tone to the human voice. As Peter approached the room, he could see crowds of people standing and talking with each other. There was a cylinder-shaped platform positioned in the center of the room. When the Captain arrived, dressed in Formal Uniform attire, he immediately got everyone's attention. White jacket with gold trim. Five stars on the left breast, with the logo Grand Central (GC) just below it. Lightweight, casual attire was given at Boarding, but Peter hadn't changed since they hadn't left port yet.

"Ladies and Gentlemen. May I have your attention, please?" A voice came over the speaker system.

The Captain stepped up to a circular platform. It would rotate slowly 360 degrees, allowing the entire room to see him at some point during his welcoming. They would sit all around the rotating platform. During ship construction, the room's concept was for permanent long-term homesteaders residing in the Fortress. GC prided itself on its innovative concepts.

Sound system Speakers surrounded the spherical space, delivering perfect, high-quality sound with virtually no echo.

A quiet voice behind Peter spoke as the man on the platform explained the ship's layout beyond their quarters.

"My name is Raymond Taylor, a man whispered behind Peter.

"Hi Raymon, my name is Peter Sullivan." Looking down at the small man.

"Sullivan, I've heard of you. Are you an astronomer?"

"You could say that," Peter replied sarcastically with a smile. "I dabble in many fields."

"I'm called the data geek around here," Ray said.

Peter raised an eyebrow in a festive mode. "I wouldn't take it personally."

"Oh no, Ray said. I gave myself that title."

25

"I see," Peter replied.

"You'll love the Captain's welcome speech. He's a great guy. It's customary for Captain Zeager to welcome us all this way."

With palms touching, fingers extended, holding close to the breast, they all bowed respectfully and exclaimed, "Namaste." And the Captain continued.

"Now, I want to welcome you all and thank you for your strong commitment to the success of this Mission."

"I am sure all of you have been inspected, dissected, and checked to exhaustion and I'm authorized to tell you, Grand Central is confident in their choices. Grand Central has stacked the deck in our favor. Rest assured, we have the best of the best on our ship.

You know our Mission is to colonize the new Planet. The task will not be easy. You all have your duties set once we arrive. A few of us will return to start the transport process for the remaining, or I should say for the willing. Rest assured, those of you with families left behind will have priority status and be the first to load the second trip off. It will be your job to prepare for their arrival.

A burst of low roar laughter came over the crowd.

"This ship can move over 1,000 personnel fully loaded, but our current load consists of what GC has set to establish a base camp. Two hundred altogether, so consider yourselves privileged. I know you all know the routine of long-term space travel by now. Study your manuals, and know your duties. We will be departing tomorrow, so get a good rest. As a reminder, the ship will initially accelerate quickly, so button down all lightweight belongings.

A small man in a white apron jumped on stage and whispered in Paul's ear.

"Oh, the Captain exclaimed. Our chef has just informed me that the formal restaurant is now officially open. You are all welcome to reserve a table within a limited capacity. I hear it's nice. The establishment will continue to provide as long as we agree to share the fringe benefit. They only asked not to reserve for everyday use. It's not an issue for us, but the second iteration will be required to alternate the two establishments to even the Graveforce."

Being an informal type, Peter preferred the smorgasbord atmosphere of the cafeteria but thought he might pop in to see the difference. It was GC's bonus for added comfort and to break up the monotony of prolonged travel.

The extra cost was hopefully worth the extravagance. Unlike the cafeteria, it offered tables, servers, and a menu.

Chapter 6

Departure

The following day, the halls were buzzing with activity. Some were exploring the ship while others were at their assigned stations. As the vessel detached from its port, one experienced the exuberant feeling of floating until the ship's engines kicked in. Over the intercom came the voice of the Captain.

"All personnel, brace to engage."

Sarah grabbed the rail along the hall as the Ship's Artificial Gravity tugged her arms from the sudden movement.

The intercom came on once again.

"Sorry for the jolt, everyone, but it beats having to briefly strap in and turn off the AG. We shouldn't have to do this again."

One hour later, eventually getting her space legs, Sarah made it to the administrative offices a little shaken but quickly adjusted. The last month had been stressful and tiring with all the procedures she had endured.

"We are finally on our way." She thought. Sarah had concluded that the Physician's assistant job was not that easy. The extreme stiffness of muscles and sore joints accompanying space flight were new to her young body.

"They must have the gravity force adjusted wrong." She thought.

Sarah nonchalantly browsed the personnel list, hoping to find a massage therapist somewhere in the roster. They hadn't listed the professions of all personnel in the database unless they were essential to the Mission. She was hoping that medical supplements, like therapists, were considered essential.

Glancing back at the boarding sequence, she noticed something strange. *What's going on here?* Sarah thought. A Lisa Sullivan appeared. Sullivan... Sulivan... she spoke in a whisper. Lisa S--volunteer---. GC had selected volunteers on an individual merit basis for this initial trip.

"Could it be?" she thought, "*Wait! She stopped herself. Peter Sullivan! The one with a face that's easy to remember.*" Sarah found herself thinking out loud. "This must be the Girl married to Professor Sullivan." She commented under her breath.

"Are you talking to me?" Doctor Miller asked as he entered the room.

"Not sure," she replied. "But we may have a stowaway."

"Better inform the Captain," Jason exclaimed.

"Oh, I will. First, let me think about this."

It was too obvious. This situation did not need Sahrha's psychic abilities.

"*I remember her being a friendly, pleasant woman.*" She thought to herself. "*She told me her husband was involved in an exclusive project. She told me how much of a family man he was and how their children were his priority.*

Mrs. Sullivan seemed like a brilliant woman. I'm sure she's capable of something like this. She has probably found a way to bring those children she bragged about with her." Sarah knew GC had not accepted children on this maiden voyage. "*She somehow must have snuck on board. Good for her,*" Sarah thought. "*I would have done the same.*"

"What do you need to think about?" Jason exclaimed.

"Oh, nothing. I think I know what's going on. I'll take care of it." Sarah replied.

"*I wonder if Peter knows of this.*" She thought.

******

Peter slept surprisingly well despite the rumored side effects. He wanted to get out and meet some crew today, especially Dr. Strauss. Peter and his wife had read the Doctor's book on DNA cloning, which intrigued them both. The well-known Biologists had successfully cloned several lab animals and even managed gene splicing in some cases. Doctor Strauss oversaw the miniature cattle section of the ship. The smaller animals would be easier to contain on a spaceship. William was more than happy to join the roster when asked. To be able to put his passion for practical use was something he'd dreamed of. He was glad GC had finally realized his potential and asset to society.

The Mission

It seemed the general public turned away from his creations for their practicality. "*They didn't understand, that's all,*" he would say. After achieving his doctoral status, it gave him a license to pursue his passion. To Bill, his work was essential to their species. In some cases, it prolonged the life span of the animal.

As Peter rounded the hallway, he saw a tall man with slightly greying hair talking to a woman.

"Dr. Strauss?" Peter spoke.

"Good morning," Bill replied.

"My name is Peter Sullivan."

"How do you do, Mr. Sullivan," Bill replied and reached to shake his hand.

"This is Mary. She's the ship's records keeper." Bill replied.

"How do you do, Mary?" Peter reached out to touch her hand.

"Listen, gentlemen, I've got to go, I'm meeting Raymon. He says it's urgent. Nice to meet you, sir."

"Likewise."

"I loved your book DNA Cloning." Peter quickly replied.

"Thank you, bring it by sometime. I'll sign it."

"So, tell me, Mr. Sullivan, what's your area of expertise? What did you do for a living before you sold your soul to the Mission?"

"I was a Professor at the university. I taught Astronomy. I also dabble in psychology."

"Oh," Bill said with a look of surprise. "Psychology, Now, that's a subject I've never considered."

"Peter quickly replied I'm currently working with the Navigation crew."

"Oh, sure," Bill replied. "This old universe is full of hurdles. Thank God for navigators."

"Yes, it's mainly ship guidance from unknown restrictions, but knowing the stars is helpful to determine placement given such a vast road to travel," Peter replied. "I predict our coordinates; the navigation guys take it from there. We often work in tandem with each other." Peter replied, trying to impress his idol.

They entered Bill's office and chatted about different subjects. The ship, the Captain, and the diverse crew until it became apparent that it was time to go to work. Peter felt secure in the idea that Bill and he had somehow bonded.

Making the rounds, having that psychology blood in his veins, and being the curious type that he was, he wanted to pick some more brains. He decided to connect with engineering. When Peter walked up, Lennard was busy talking to Raymond, the data geek.

"Maybe you can help me," Raymond was asking Lenord.

Lenn replied, "I'll try. What's up?"

"I was just wondering, do you have the Mission's logs I asked you to keep for me? The ones before departure. The ground-level logs?"

"Of course, they are secure if that's what you mean."

"No, no," Ray replied. "I overheard some passengers talking, saying the Mission logs had been tampered with, causing a re-route."

"Huh?" Lenn looked puzzled.

"You know as well as I do that passenger log entries are secured within a locked system for a reason. To alter something like that would be impossible. The consequences of that would result in a felony and be considered a threat to GC's success. That's a pretty steep claim to be making Raymon."

"Yeah, I know. That's why I need to debunk it. "

They were unaware of Peters's presence until he finally spoke up behind them.

"Hey fellows, I didn't mean to interrupt."

The two friends turned around and quickly altered the conversation in a different direction. "Oh, sorry, Ray here is just being paranoid. There will always be ones who dislike following the system and will challenge anything just for the sake of the challenge. I've seen it before." Lenn added.

"Raymond, you are overreacting and talking about GC's hard-pressed selection of professionals," Lenn said sarcastically.

"Just asking, Len."Raymon smiled.

"Gentlemen," Peter said. "I hear you wear many hats around here."

"Yep, sometimes," Raymond said.

"There will always be trouble makers. Space flight can do that to a person."

"Yeah," Raymon said. "But the way he acted, it was like he knew something we didn't."

"If he does know something, and if he's not an idiot," Lenny said. "He should know better to spread rumors. Let's not stress it right now, Ray. I'll bet it's someone trying to escape the boredom with a little controversy. Besides, I need to figure out the Duration Interval Program's aperture. Engineering wants to reset the startup time for the Ecosystem. Have you checked with Mary?"

"Not yet. I will. We're having lunch together."

The fictitious scenario that Len quickly fabricated could have very well been actual for all he knew. The records contamination was genuine and could have meant that there were real saboteurs on board, but false conclusions were non-productive at this point. Creating a rowdy, loud mouth was an easy cover to his questioning, just in case Pete overheard anything. Loud mouths were easy to deal with. It was the Tech geeks you had to worry about, and this culprit had to have been a Tech Geek. *"An easy catch for Raymon since he, too, fits in that envelope."* Lenny thought.

Raymon knew that until more information was available, he needed to keep a lid on the situation around most members since the culprit was unknown. Peter, being there at the time, made it hard to talk to Lenny, who quickly covered for him.

Ray had to talk to people to get answers, but knowing which people was the trick. Lenny felt Raymon's apprehension but had to let it go. There was *no need to stir up the Professor*, he thought.

******

Everyone loved Mary with her sweet disposition and always being mindful of other's feelings. Always willing to help, she seldom thought of herself over other's needs and often gave back more than she would take. Her records never reflected negative thoughts. You were always, without a doubt, innocent until proven guilty. She was the type that was always comfortable to be around. THAT! was Mary in a nutshell. She had an analytical way about her, and Raymon needed that analysis.

Chapter 7

COMPUTER FORENSIC'S

With nothing but idol time on their hands, in the empty arms of the black void of space, Lenn decided to Follow up on Raymon's records delima after the fact. He started checking to see if there might be any suspicious activity. He knew it wouldn't be easy to edit any previously saved data. All data information was classified. The Log site had on-screen, in small print, at the bottom of the display.

"For Grand Central Employee's use Only."

It carried a priority memory inscription key code and a personal retina check. Log Records were essential during any mission; altering them could result in criminal charges, especially now that they would be entering uncharted territory. The backup system also showed the void.

Maybe someone was trying to cover up a mistake. Possibly one that might damage one's career, Len thought. Every Mission had trip logs that followed each individual. Len already had the daily menial cataloging all the Captain's entries, but now, he had the entire crew to cross-reference. He was looking for any out-of-place data. Identification codes, in-proper language use, dates out of sequence. Verifying the validity of the data was very time-consuming until, finally, Eureka! A clue appeared! It came into sight when Len noticed that a log was tagged "important," which was odd to Len. A crew member had inserted a record with coded data, accessing the mapping system.

Lenn called his friend on the com.

"Hey Ray, have you found anything of interest."

The Mission

"Mary discovered the illegal infiltration happened while the Fortress was being stocked."

"This crew member was no ordinary crew member," Lenny said. "This guy knew what he was doing." He was impressed that the culprit entered the system anonymously.

"Somehow, this person cracked a top-priority code. It must have been an insider." Ray remarked.

Now, they just needed to find out who. See if you could catch anyone talking in casual conversation. Lenny kept an open eye and an open ear. Most of all, he wanted to know how they did it. How someone got by the security's electronic door locks, and change the database?

Lenn loved a good mystery, and this investigation was about to get interesting.

******

"Where have you been, Sarah? I needed you here." Dr. Miller exclaimed as she walked into his office.

"I had to get with Raymond. It seems they were short," she paused to see if Jason caught the reference.

"A few uniforms."

And that would involve you, how? Jason asked

"I was the one that placed the unique order for little Raymon. He's quite short, you know?"

"Well, Next time, promise me you'll wear your com unit so I can contact you when I need to."

"Okay, sorry about that. Did you need me to do something for you now?"

"No, but my com-unit was buzzing off the stand. I couldn't get anything done.

The crew fell into the routine as the virtual days moved on. There was a young man slated to help Dr. Strauss with the animals. He had been an apprentice to a cattle farmer at home. He Grew up around farmers and knew how to handle large animals. Especially the animals meant for slaughter. His expertise was butchering. He liked the idea of the hybrid beef being of more diminutive stature.

He went by the name Duane only. He kept a low profile in light of his track record, which he'd painstakingly left behind. The Mission gave him a way to change his life. To re-invent himself, he separated himself from the nickname "The Bucher," which he despised. "In profession only." He'd shout in his own defense.

He knew how to butcher cattle but didn't care to identify by that title. William wondered if *he also learned how to butcher other things, like......?* Something about Duane didn't feel right. It seemed odd that GC would have included him on the Mission, although he certainly knew his craft. It must have been a Bargain sentencing for wrongdoings back home since he was assigned to be part of the permanent crew. "*It beats going to jail.*" He thought.

"So, Duane, tell me. Has anyone informed you of the significance of our existence here on this Ship?" Bill asked, sensing the tension in the boy.

With a complete look of puzzlement on his face, Duane replied.

"No, sir."

"DANG!" Strauss replied. "Guess I'll have to wait for the next recruit. They never tell me anything. Strauss then waited for a response to his sarcasm but got nothing.

"Okay then," Bill replied.

"We need to make sure these animals stay healthy. They are what I call BOD, "Butcher on demand." I'm letting the kitchen govern that. We also need to manage their breeding. There's only so much room on this Ship for added animals."

"Tell you what. I'll need you to mark the male's chest with this oil ink. Just splatter in on. He won't mind. It marks the rump of all the females they've mounted. Then we'll know which one to watch. Once we get our quota, we'll need to separate them. We don't want to see more than four females marked at a time.

Also, let me know if you see any animals limping. We'll need to march them through the chemical trough to kill the hoof rot picked from walking in their droppings. We need to stay on that, but sometimes it's hard to do when other demands take priority. GC will partition more on the second run since you'll need more help at total capacity.

I'm not laying this all on you, Duane. These are shared responsibilities."

Although he knew Duane would eventually be in charge of the farm.

"I'll train you on the automatic milking stations. This system is awesome." Bill added.

"We're high-tech here. Also, let me know if an Animal becomes sic. You'll learn from their actions. I'll be able to diagnose the problem through

The Mission

the multi-database and hopefully treat it in time. Quite often, success depends on the time it takes to address a virus, so keep an open eye.

Their existence was anything but meager. As Bill put it, feeding the ship family and keeping them happy and healthy was necessary for space travel. Meat eaters wanted their protein, and Bill was there to accommodate. This was the first in space flight history to include live animals in the manifest, and Bill was the proud pioneer. He always kept a stern disposition about the project. To Bill, it was the most essential part of the Mission itself.

Duane was a young man. Mission Control asked Bill to overlook his slight temper, which made itself known a few years back in a shopping mall when he took an assaulter to the floor, breaking his nose. The guy pressed charges, claiming he was physically accosted.

No witnesses were willing to come forward in Duane's defense. He might have gotten a lesser conviction if the victim had come to the court and mentioned the trauma and the stressful damage the assaulter had inflicted on him. As it was, Duane got 30-day jail time to cool off. The Judge of that particular court that day was not known to be lenient. In Duane's own defense, he told the Judge, "*No one had the right to demoralize another for personal gain.*" In a public setting, the derogatory badgering of a person was the breaking point for Duane. He acted on impulse when he intervened. The victim thanked him later.

Duane loved it on the Ship. In time, one could see the change in his disposition. He started to open up once he got out of reach from the tyranny of Poseidon. He was recruited with the knowledge of working the Ship for four consecutive migrations and passing the farm on to the next recruit if and when he is released. He could also remain for all trips If he chose. Eventually, his age would catch up, and he would have to pass on his position, which suited him fine since he was doing what he loved. He planned on staying on board even after the Mission was complete. By then, the Ship would have become a homestead.

The large monitor screen of the Bridge flashed a message that read Captain Zeager, Private.

"I'll take it in my quarters," Paul said as he headed for the elevator.

"What's this about?" He thought. *So soon into the Mission, was he already getting private calls from Mission Control?* They had gotten word of an intruder, and it concerned them. It wasn't that the Mission was at risk, but the technology had been breached, and competitors were always willing to steal working technology, some for evil purposes.

"We are on it, Sir. I have the best investigators working it night and day.

Chapter 8

SET ADRIFT

Lisa waited patiently in room 313. *It was only going to be for two years.* She thought. She would do whatever it took to stay hidden from the Captain if Peter wanted that. Keeping the family together was her priority. Getting the room's keycode was a Godsend. She had neglected to plan for that, but it came in a way she least expected.

The navigational computer system would re-route slightly, creating a diversion while she located Peter in the enormous ship. It Kept the constables busy tracking down the glitch while she hunted for her husband. Traversing the corridors unnoticed would make it easier with the uniform she received. It should have made for a good blend, although she noticed many did not wear the required dress. Most were still in their city clothes.

Initially, she thought she'd stage a casual meeting with Peter in the mess hall or some public spot on the ship, but she decided it was best to do it privately. She was getting a little anxious as she waited. As long as they were together, it was the only thing that mattered to her.

Her heart raced when she heard the door code sound. She held her breath as time momentarily stopped as he entered.

"LISA?!" He gasped. "Oh my God, sweetheart! You're here?"

"I couldn't tell you before now," Lisa explained.

"I don't even want to know how - this is amazing."

They embraced, and Peter was in heaven for the first time in months. He thought to himself.

The Mission

I never knew how good it felt to hold Lisa. I was always too busy to notice.
They both cried together, holding each other for hours.
"Sweetheart, I am so sorry for leaving you and the……..,"
He paused for a moment,
"Where are the kids?"
"They're probably exploring the ship somewhere. Don't worry, honey. There are so many casually dressed people on this ship. They'll blend in.
"I had help once I got here." There is an incredibly kind woman on board. She gave me this uniform and showed us to your room.
"Ummu," Peter said, holding his chin, "You must be talking about Sarah, but you won't need the uniform."
"I see that now." Lisa smiled.
"Maybe she thought you'd be better posing as an officer."
"She said she remembered me from the museum," Lisa replied.

******

Life is good, Peter thought as he held Lisa as close as he could without hurting her. He prayed,
"Dear God," he prayed. "Thank you for bringing us this wonderful blessing." As Lisa squeezed him back, they cried tears of joy.
While Lisa explained her method of getting to the ship, Peter was impressed with his wife's abilities.
"Why did you keep it from me?"
"I didn't want you to worry. You had enough on your mind at the time. I started planning three months ago."
"I Love you so much, sweetheart," she said as they slowly fell asleep. Later, the kids silently slipped in for the night, unnoticed. Sarah had supplied single cots for the kids. It was tight, but they were all together.

******

She had convinced one of the seasoned shuttle pilots into secretly riding up during one of the many supply runs. Her beauty may have helped with that request. Then, it was a matter of hiding until personnel arrived and getting her name and the kids' aliases onto the roster. She knew the rapport Peter shared with GC was good, so replacing his name with hers, she'd hoped, would not draw much attention. Luckily for her, the shuttle pilot knew how to temporally pause the computer, allowing Lisa to sneak into the system's back door and rearrange the names to reflect theirs.

"We're too far out to return home with a shuttle, and we're all together. God is on our side, for sure. Let's go find the kids." Peter replied.

"Okay, They are down on the first floor."

******

Grand Central's Flying Fortress employed extra personnel for all departments. GC offered volunteers, odd jobs, and some essential positions with on-the-job training. All one needed was the right attitude and the ability to follow orders. It worked out just right for the kids. Lisa listed the kids as two years older so as not to alert the others. She later found that being incognito wasn't necessary.

******

Months passed, and Lisa was already helping with some of the patients who visited the Psychology ward that Peter was running on the side. She was scheduling appointments and following through with any medication she was allowed to allocate. She occasionally consulted patients whenever Peter was too busy searching the universe for the new home, which had lately become his priority. However, the psych ward was currently at a minimum.

When Peter finally spotted their Planet, the crew immediately celebrated. The restaurant always stayed open, so it was alive, with crew members constantly beaming. There was a festive atmosphere throughout the ship. Anxiety turned to anticipation.

The small Planet had a hazy atmosphere covering the entire surface. It was just as they had anticipated from home. The rotation was similar to their home Planet, and the distance to its mother star made it habitable. Finally hovering over the new world, the Mission crew prepared for disembarkment. As the Pilots prepared their ships, they loaded shuttles with supplies and personal belongings. The haze seemed to linger and cover everything. They were finally close enough to send a probe to check the season.

The Mission

******

Herman Towers came over the ship's intercom.

"Captain Zeager! Please report to the Bridge."

Herman was standing in front of the monitor screen when the Captain entered. He was a large man in comparison. The entire crew respected and welcomed his position of second in command. His years of experience spanned several decades. Had it not been for Paul Zeager's impeccable track record and years of experience, Herman would have been chosen to Captain the Ship.

"What's up, Towers?" He exclaimed.

"First of all," Herman replied with frustration.

"The alert system of this ship does not work! I was lucky you were able to hear the intercom when you did. We have a significant problem here, Captain. One of our planetary probes has caused the Planet to light up."

"How could that be?" The Captain asked.

"Not sure yet. Everything was fine until we sent a chemical analysis probe to check the atmosphere. The scout probe exploded on impact. Then, the whole Planet lit up like an internal candle."

"And you're saying our probe had something to do with it?"

"All I can do at this point is assume," Herman said. "We can't be sure, but the Planet's atmosphere and our probe exhaust could have been the wrong chem-mix. It all happened quickly, but it looks as if the probe might have initiated an enormous explosion."

"Sir, if I may?" Peter Sullivan interrupted as he entered the Bridge. I believe we should be preparing to retreat as soon as possible. A planet explosion of this size, at this range, could kill us all."

"Magnify," the Captain ordered.

From a close view, one could see thick clouds hurling in all directions, almost canceling the Planets's glow.

"Gentleman, we've done all the damage we could ever do here. God forgive us."

The Captain exclaimed, "Let's get out of here!"

Raymond threw the compulsive drive into hyper, 20,000k, maximum speed, knocking the unprepared crew off their feet.

Shortly after the drive engaged, the Planet's explosion force caught up and propelled the ship into a spin, throwing everything not nailed down into the air. The gyro system took a while to correct itself. Badly limping from the tumble, Raymond made his way to the engine room through the rubble resulting from the tumbling ship.

"Ray! Are you there?" The Captain shouted over the problematic intercom system, hoping someone heard the call.

"Taylor here, Sir. Two main engines are down, and we're now on emergency power." The Captain then hailed all posts for a report.

"Doctor Miller?" The Captain yelled into the mic.

After a short pause of silence….

"I'm sorry, Captain," Sarah replied, "but we're having a sudden rush of patients down here."

"How's the Doctor?"

I think his leg is broken. He took quite a fall."

"I'm fine!" The Doctor could be heard yelling over the COM unit in the background.

Due to the faulty intercom, the Captain headed off for engineering on the run, quickly checking in with Strauss. The animals were shaken but not damaged. Duane could handle them.

Raymond, being of small stature, was tattered but functional. He had his hands full with the aftermath. He met the Captain as they approached.

"Raymond! Are you okay?"

"Seem to be, Sir, a sprained ankle, maybe."

"How are we looking down here?" The Captain asked the mechanic on duty.

"We lost the number 4 engine. Something flew into it and cracked the housing. It's leaking fluid. Two are salvageable, and One is still running. I got the crew working on it, but it may take a while.

GC did provide replacement parts for the Mission, but engine casings were not one of them.

"We can run with the one for now, but it will be slow going. You have to be careful not to overwork it. I'd hate to be adrift out here."

"I'm having to shut off parts of section C," Ray said as he adjusted the console knobs.

"There's a Pressure leak."

"Understand, Raymond, do your best."

The Mission

As the Captain entered the Doctor's quarters, he clenched his fists. The loss of personnel was his responsibility.

"We lost seven volunteers, Sir, and more wounded keep arriving." Dr. Miller spoke as the Captain entered the room.

"Are you okay, Jason?" Paul asked, giving a heavy sigh.

"I'm okay. After Sarah reset my leg, bless her heart. I can work from this wheelchair well enough. I'm best as a consultant here anyway. Sarah has made a list of the injured.

******

Planetary implosions were non existant in any GC's manuals.

Peter had seen implosions years before. At the same time, amateurs were looking for new planets. The Universities had a dedicated department that would evaluate profound deep space events. They found that dying stars gave plenty of warning signs years in advance before their death, ruling out a spontaneous explosion like this. They had never known a Plane to do that. There was a category in GC's Specifications book entitled (Unknown) subtitled (Unexpected career casualty), but it did not list world explosions.

In their hast to launch, many scenarios were unknown. "The Captain concluded in his documentation that "This will be recorded in any forthcoming manual, as a cautionary warning to execute substantial research before subjecting hardware (probes) in an unknown environment." Luckily, the event spared them the devastation but left them with the trauma. The Captain logged the exploding Planet as a Level II disaster. Which meant Heavy damage, but still able enough to limp along in search of the nearest available retreat.

"May God be with us." He prayed.

******

Work crews were busy around the virtual clock. Everyone had extra work added to their schedules. Everyone that was still able to help would pitch in. Outside the ship, spacewalkers were examining the exterior. Sensors were missing along with cameras used for visual, and an array of hull damage that left holes in the surface. The ship was sturdy for the most part. It was the interior that took most of the damage. Most of the crew's physical damage was due to the explosion's force and the ship's tumble through space.

The top priority was radio transmitters. They'd lost the main signal booster needed to transmit far distances. Without it, the radio would be useless to contact home.

Chapter 9

Rehabilitation

Aside from being the charismatic diplomat, Paul's second-in-command was an excellent pilot. As he jettisoned the shuttle, he could immediately see the blast's effect, leaving scars and streaks of debris clinging to the ship's surface. Through closer inspection, he decided that most of the exterior was in relatively good condition. Aside from the crack along the rear Section, it was still in flyable condition. Being a strong man in nature, he couldn't pretend to ignore his despair from what he saw.

Herman spoke into the close-range intercom system from a shuttle outside the ship. "Looks as if the most massive damage occurred over Section C."

"Affirmative?" The Captain replied.

"Sir. We'll have to keep that Section closed."

"All right, Herman. Assess all the damages and bring me a report. I'll alert Engineering."

"Will do, Captain," Herman replied. He would identify the hot spots and let engineering diagnose the damage.

******

The blast had thrown the nav-line into total confusion. It was unknown where the Fortress inertia came to rest until Raymond could get the coordinate system working again.

Peter Sullivan had been scanning the area for nearby planets but could find none. He used the RBT (Really Big Telescope), positioned just above the main engineering deck, to look into deep space. The tedious job brought him no success in the weeks that followed. He felt it odd that he couldn't find a single star. Had they fallen into some space void? He'd heard about these portions of black space. These voids were supposedly a vacuum portal. Pulling in dead stars and planets. There was a common scenario circulating at the University. They called it "House Cleaning." Sweeping the dirty Universe under the rug,,, or in this case, into a hole.

Peter shuttered to think, "*Had their worst nightmare come true?*"

The ship's intercom crackled with static.

All officers report to the boardroom!

******

Chairs quickly filled as personnel filed into the room. Paul Zeager was waiting at the podium. The Captain wasted no time in addressing the very talkative crowd. They all were eager to hear the prognoses.

"Everyone, Thanks for the quick response." He started.

"You all know the circumstances of a level II disaster. I am embarrassed to announce our targeted Planet is gone. The implosion was our fault. It seems a vulnerable element existed in the Planet's atmosphere that we did not detect from home. Our probe's exhaust penetrated its core, causing a massive pressure build-up. Let us pray that there were no living creatures there. If there were life, know it happened quickly. They couldn't have suffered long. Let us all pray."

Paul bowed his head, as did the entire room.

"*Dear God of our universe forgives us. We are your creations, but we do not have the wisdom you possess. If we are to be held responsible, we'll do what is required. We put our souls in your hands. Please have mercy. We were mistaken in our judgment, God. We are your humble servants.*"

"Amen." was heard by people.

Paul continued speaking.

"The explosion of the Planet has hurled us into a deep space. We have no reference to how far we traversed before the ship finally came to rest. I'm assuming the casualties are all accounted for. I thank God for the lives he spared and ask him to be with the ones we lost."

The Mission

"Amen," was chanted in the crew. We will survive with the help of this ship's talented crew. Thank you all for that."

"Peter Sullivan, our Astronomer, has been working day and night searching for an alternative planet. We've fortunately been spared one good engine. Our ship can sustain life indefinitely; Our propulsion system will carry us on but at a different capacity. Have patience."

"Captain! Sir," Herman Towers spoke up. "Also, we lost some good men. I'll cross-train the essential positions after our loss in Section C."

The Captain shook his head. "Thanks."

******

After the unfortunate mishap, the entire ship went on emergency procedures. The vessel ran quite well, considering that they had lost key personnel. As it was, many, without questioning, adjusted for the loss, doubling their responsibilities.

"What do you have, Ray?" Paul asked.

"Sir, we're receiving what I believe to be a stress call, but it's intermittent. They keep reaching out. I tried to reply, but we must not be reaching them. It sounds like they are saying,

"Mother, of maybe Monster. But I'm not sure. It's a weak signal, hard to make out."

"Have you tried all channels?"

"Yes, with no success."

It seemed the Mission had stumbled upon a galaxy close enough to receive external radio signals. Friend or foe, it was a comforting sound regardless.

"Humm, monster? I wonder what that means." The Captain asked.

"I know what it means to me!" Ray replied. "Not Good."

"I agree, Raymon, but you're hearing from a different culture and species with completely different concepts. Let's not make any pre-judgements. Keep on it, and see if you can't make out their language. They may have a code we need to break."

"Let's hope not, Captain. Secret Codes equate to covert communications and war."

******

Almost as suddenly as the black sounded them, leaving them adrift for days. Peter's telescope suddenly filled with stars.

He could see millions when he focused on a tiny section of space.

"Now that's more like it!" He said. Turning to focus the lens.

He reached out as far as the scope could take him. When galaxies started looking alike, he stopped and contemplated his positioning. *He had to dig deeper,* he thought. *Observe their movements and reactions relative to each other.* Hours passed with no luck.

Almost falling asleep several times with the repetitiveness while sitting still, he turned in for the night.

"Hi honey, any luck?" Lisa said as he entered their home quarters.

"Good news and bad news. What do you want first?"

She looked at him with a lowered brow and half grin.

"The stars are back. Just like before."

"Peter! That's Great News." She remarked with excitement.

"But it isn't easy. It's like looking for a needle in a haystack. It's a whole different thing when you're looking for planets out of necessity." Peter replied with a heavy sigh.

"Anything interesting happening at the center?" he asked.

"No, maybe a few anxieties, but nothing beyond that. I'm doing my best."

"I know you are sweetheart. Reassure the patients that they are in the best hands."

******

The following day, with a new perspective, he noticed a peculiar, somewhat docile star system. He thought it was only a little less active than any other system. Eight planets were orbiting one star. One Planet drew his attention more so. Calibrated focusing made it clear that the land masses were surrounded by water. This suddenly raised Peter's blood pressure. Excitement engulfed him as he looked even closer.

Further investigating showed it was rotating its host star at the same rate as Poseidon orbited its host. Peter immediately alerted the Bridge and asked permission to send a probe. Captain suggested to engineering that pulling back some before they do might be wise this time.

The Mission

The probe's reading returned oxygen hydrogen with a carbon dioxide atmosphere. *Could this be?* He thought. *It was too good to be true.* He sent another probe to be sure. His excitement caused him to almost fall off his chair. "I need to see the Captain!" he said without hesitation, heading to the elevator. He paced the elevator floor with anticipation until it reached the top.

Suddenly, the door opened, and he exploded through it.

"Captain!" He exclaimed. "I may have found us a home. It appears as if it exists in the inhabitable zone of its master star."

"Tell me it's a level IV, and I'll promote your wife." He said with a sarcastic, happy sound.

Not that she needed promoting necessarily. She had become a valued crew member in the last few months.

"All eight planets orbited the host within their own radius, and If my calculations are correct, the third one out is suitable for life. It's slightly smaller than ours, so the gravitational pull should be less.

Its core is not solid, so the rotation is slower, probably causing longer days and nights. If I'm reading this correctly, this Planet could be our home." He said, being as optimistic as possible since optimism was desperately needed now.

"Good news, finally!" The Captain exclaimed. "There never was enough hours in a day back home." He said, with a grin on his face. "Let's see what we got when we get there. Get with Lenny with the coordinates. He'll set the course."

******

"From our current location, at this slower pace, I figured it would take at least six months," Lenny replied.

"Good news, heh? Peter replied.

"I'm just happy to have you as my scout, Peter. It's good to have something to look forward to again.

"Scout?" Peter thought. "I like the sound of that. It looks like I'm also wearing several hats during this Mission."

There was no mention in any initiation documents, but Peter felt that one unspoken criterion for acceptance on the Mission was to be capable of diversity. Peter had excelled in just about anything he attempted. Lisa would refer to him as "Her Renaissance Man."

******

There was word circulating on board of a miracle. Morale was returning. Extremists had been exaggerating anguish after the last disaster, so the news was welcomed. Peter became an overnight superstar in the eyes of the Mission. Once again, their savior provided hope that the people of Poseidon would survive and continue. Their civilization would carry on.

******

Dr. Strauss was dining alone when Paul entered the café'.

"Captain, have a seat."

After the excitement had slightly calmed and things had returned to normal, the Captain decided to eat with the enlisted that night. Herman Towers joined them shortly after.

"Herman!"Captain exclaimed. What brings you out tonight?

"The question is," Herman replied, "what brought you out? I come here every night."

Four months had passed since the Planet's discovery, and the crew was starting to get anxious. Excitement was beginning to build, so using the restaurant was an excellent place to gather and relax the anxiety. The new Planet was visible from the ship's position, and the land mass was a welcome site. Just like the ones on Poseidon.

The Captain ordered a shuttle scouting to investigate. Sarah Clark then entered the café.

"Gentlemen, may I join you?"

She eagerly circled the table and sat beside the Captain without a reply or hesitation. She was bubbling with anticipation.

"Captain, I formally request a seat on the first shuttle down."

"Has the Doctor agreed with this?"

"He's a little reluctant but agrees with me."

"So inform me," The Captain spoke up, "how would it be beneficial for you to go first?"

"In case there are hostilities, I might be useful."

"Could you read the mind of an alien?" Towers snidely commented.

"I don't read them. I feel them." Sarah replied. "I could warn you of hostility before it happened."

The Mission

"It might be helpful since we don't know what we may encounter." The Captain quickly replied.

"Thank you, Captain. I promise I won't let you down." She said as she jumped from the table and hurried away.

"I said it Might be!" the Captain yelled as she rushed away.

"Guess she didn't want to eat after all," Strouse commented.

******

Sarah's clairvoyance branched out in different directions. Sometimes, she would use inanimate objects owned by a missing person to help locate them. She attempted a Psychic crime solver business years before, but the clients weren't that susceptible to the idea. It turned out to be less lucrative than she'd hoped. She had produced enough evidence and helped solve enough crimes to convince anyone she was not a hoax. But the lawyers labeled it witchery and inadmissible in court. She suspected they had alternative reasons. She knew it was her intuitions that they were afraid of. As she put it. *"It's hard to argue with facts."*

She finally turned to administrative work to survive, leaving the door open for part-time sleuthing.

She seemed to have an uncanny ability to feel spirits, more so when the living relatives were available to consult with. She was often able to feel the bond that existed between them.

That was Sarah's initial contact with the Good Doctor. It seemed his wife's spirit had stayed behind and was a little lost. He asked Sarah to help her to find her way.

Since childhood, Sarah has been able to predict the future and sometimes feel others' thoughts.

******

The Captain disagreed with GC's decision to keep The Sulivan's pre-graduating children from the first mission. He did, however, agree with Doctor Miller regarding health checks. Lisa had boarded incognito without going through Medical. Paul thought it best to quarantine her and the kids until the Doctor could examine them. Doctor Miller understood the dangers of the fatal virus that would hide within some organic immune systems, and Peter's family was no exception. Everyone needed testing.

"I'll bring them in." the Doctor said. He had patched up most victims of the planet explosion and arranged for the burials on the new planet. He might have some extra time on his hands now. I'll get the paperwork in order tonight."

Sarah visited the Sullivan family to inform them. Lisa never got to know Captain Zeager that well. She would have to be the one to explain the computer glitch to the Captain in case he needed to charge her for illegalities. She was the one responsible for altering the logs. It was a relief to Zeager to finally know the cause of the confusion. The innocence of it would touch him. As Saraha explained it. "It was done out of love for the family." Legal or not, her testimony was enough for Paul to ignore the legalities.

Chapter 10

ADAPTATION

Attention! Attention! All Personnel prepare for dis-embarkment!

Peter Sullivan was never one to hit the ground running, and this moment was no exception. His eyes were blurry, stumbling, and confused. At first, he thought he was still dreaming.

The sleep shift was total confusion when the ship alarm instructed them to abandon the ship. The way the alert system guided them to the shuttles that came without warning was even more confusing.

Has anyone seen my wife?

Peter kept asking the frantic crew as they ran in all directions, looking back as if he was crazy. His heart racing, he caught up with the panicked crowd.

"Was he crazy? His wife was with him, wasn't she?"

Through the commotion, Peter quickly realizes it isn't a dream and starts feeling the urgency.

"My God, we have been attacked!" There was smoke filling the halls. The walls were hot to the touch, using them for guidance through the thick haze.

"Please move along, sir," a voice came behind him. "Before we all choke!"

"Where is Lisa?!" He kept repeating.

"Sorry, Sir, I don't know her." Another one claimed as he hurriedly passed by.

Heading to the cargo launch area, hoping to find her and the kids waiting for him, he tripped and fell to the floor.

"I must find my family!" He continued to limp as runners passed by him. Some of the shuttles had already started their route to the Planet. His family was nowhere in sight. Peter panicked for a moment, then started asking around. The intercom system was in the worst shape. You could hardly understand the message. Peter decided to wait to load until the last shuttle in case Lisa showed up. The main ship shook, with sounds of cracking during all the commotion. Smoke billowed into the Cargo bay. It was time to leave! He boarded the last shuttle to jettison the mothership, not a minute too soon. Looking back, Peter could see the main ship, their oasis in the heavens, falling apart and breaking into pieces.

"If they are anywhere, he thought, they must be on the Planet by now. God protect them." He prayed.

Being on the last shuttle put Peter with the second in command Herman Towers, Doctor Miller, and William Strauss.

Raymond and Lennard were strapped in the shuttle's rear, sitting side by side. The Captain was directly in front of Peter.

"Ray and Lenn were lucky," he thought. *"They always seem to find each other. I wish I had their luck."*

As they plummeted to the Planet's surface, Peter bowed his head.

"Please, keep my family safe," He prayed.

One could start to feel the gravity of the Planet taking hold of the shuttle as they neared the surface. It was no smooth ride after that. Peter looked at the Captain.

What happened? He asked.

"Pirates!" Paul exclaimed.

The attack came in full force. Its stealthy arrival gave the Mission no time to respond, destroying half the sleeping quarters and some of the Bridge.

"I saw them on the overhead monitors as I sounded the alarms." The Captain explained. The leader tried explaining something to me, but we had little time to chat." Paul explained sarcastically. "It wouldn't have made any difference; the language was alien, and we were going down. Maybe he had an itchy trigger finger and was trying to apologize for a premature hit, but I greatly doubt that, since Pirates do not feel remorse."

"Are you sure it was Pirates?"

"A Pirate will always shoot, without bothering to ask questions. To a Pirate, everyone is an enemy. They never even gave us a warning. Pirates don't fight fair. They must have figured that we were not a ship of war, that they

The Mission

would get no resistance. Unfortunately, Our firepower was docked, so any chances of a retaliation were nil. We were unprepared for this. It was my fault for letting my guard down."

Assuming all responsibility, the Captain was demoralized. His track record and graces surrounding him throughout his life, had now deserted him. The Mission was a disaster, and Paul blamed himself. He felt he should have been constantly alert but had gotten complacent after discovering the new Planet.

Sensing the Captain's remorse, Peter encouraged him.

"This is not your fault, Captain. God is with us now. God knows what is best for us. After all, he put you in charge. Mistakes are a part of life. We all trust and admire you, Sir, and that will never change."

With a forced smile, the Captain replied, "Thank you for that."

"Believe me, Captain, we will need you more than ever after this. You are, and have always been our beacon."

As the shuttle spiraled down, the pilot exclaimed, "We're getting HOT!" Looking out his portal, Peter saw some shuttles catching fire and exploding. "*Save us from this!*" someone yelled. *"After all we've been through, please don't let it end this way."* Peter was Gripping his chair, praying for his family. He thought he could hear the words. "*I will protect them.*"

The small ship landed softly since the pilot was unfamiliar with the different gravitational pull and overcompensated his approach. Shuttles dotted the countryside. There was no time to coordinate a fail-safe escape route. The way it happened, they were lucky to make it off the ship in time. Peter's shuttle managed to stay together with a few others.

Given the nature of the chaotic exit, Peter prayed that everyone landed somewhat close to each other within a kilometer. Peter hoped that Lisa would be near. As soon as the dust settled, he would start his search.

The people exited the ships safely on the surface, but more chaos commenced while everyone frantically screamed for friends as they came together. There was no reply when Peter yelled for his family.

Luckily, all shuttles had been pre-stocked with supplies needed for survival before leaving the Fortress. Initially, the survivors slept inside the shuttles to escape the cold of the mountain they landed on.

******

The Captain wasted no time in calling a meeting.

He spoke loud enough for all to hear. He needed to reassure them that he was still their Captain and willing to serve them, although he also required the reassurance himself. Speaking over the confusion, he addressed the crowd.

"People, can I have your attention?"

Adrenaline was racing as some became frantic, but he knew the crowd always listened whenever he spoke.

"I suggest we slow down a little until we all get used to the oxygen level and gravity. I don't think overexerting ourselves right away would be too productive."

"Captain, there are cities below us." Someone yelled.

"And," he added. "It's probably a good idea to remain out of reach. At least until we discover if the locals are allies or adversaries."

The Captain scanned the area. "Has anyone seen Sarah Clark?" he asked.

"Here I am, Captain. I'll be checking the inventory of both survivors and supplies." She announced.

"We lost quite a lot in the Fortress," Herman replied.

******

Later that same evening, a lone scouting shuttle returned with pressing news.

"We've spotted two crashed shuttles. Sir, We scanned the area but detected no life forms nearby."

Paul understood casualties, but this one was hard for him. It was unexpected. Being caught defenseless was his biggest fear. The first line of business was to secure the area. Being somewhat de-sensitized to death from his service days and experiences, he couldn't help but beat himself up for the loss of this tragedy. The Mission was supposed to be a peaceful endeavor. A new hope. He was sure the home planet would undoubtedly re-coup, but the innocent hopefuls and families left behind would suffer for years. This was, after all, a Mission of no return.

Setting up camp was a top priority. There seemed to be enough crude material around to start building. They fortified the main house using shuttles to move large rocks and trees. The crew worked round the clock as the season's longer days moved in. They were clearing areas for crops and moving the existing stones into place. They made heavy work quick and easy. Shuttles were so busy during the setup they could no longer be used for search and rescue, so Peter could only wait and hope that his family found him. There had been no shuttles other than their own flying overhead, so his faith in finding any family was slowly declining.

Peter's professional status had changed since the Cosmos was no longer a concern. The library, which disinterested him completely, consisted of titles [Diplomacy versus Manipulation.] [Self-awareness for the New Life), and [Outdoor Survival Challenges.] These are challenges that GC must have thought would be needed in the new world. He finally decided to focus on his experience in psychology. Plenty of people's condolences were required, and with his kind heart, he was always there to lend a shoulder. His methods were simple. They believed in Karma and accepted both favorable and unfavorable events, which would eventually yield positive results. Peter felt that the Preaching of God lent itself to this reckoning.

Everyone helped build the base camp by assisting carpenters and masons. It was slowly materializing. The material was easy enough to deliver. The assembly took time, and with it being grievous work, they reserved a day of rest.

Then, Peter started a condolence group for those who lost friends and family, knowing they had lost any connection with their home base. Sympathy was not addressed there. Instead, strength and hope were the topics of most discussions. Acceptance of loss took time, he would say. It helped to have others to confide in. If you can't feel it, you can't heal it. He would often say. Each week, he would start his meeting with a prayer."

"Dear God, we put our lives and prayers in your hands. Guide us to your heaven and protect us from evil around us. Please have mercy on our souls and forgive us for our sins. We are but your humble servants. Amen"

******

The gravitational pull was much less on this new Planet, and the weather was primarily cold. Peter became the camp's psychiatrist and spiritual guidance leader, all in one. He seemed to fit into the position very well. Peter taught us that aligning the stars' planets and distances was essential to our lives. He had found his niche. He was convinced that his God was present in the entire universe, and this Planet was no exception.

God was everything to everyone, regardless of which world you were in. From his philosophical upbringing, his teaching eventually transformed from astronomy to astrology, giving meaning to the stars and their orbiting families, saying the movement of the Cosmos can affect the continuum.

He even started making predictions into the future for simple things like weather change or displacement of ideas. He knew that one Planet seemed to retrograde in its path at certain times, giving it significance to specific events.

******

There was no need for Jason Miller to change direction. He kept busy enough with new viruses that kept showing up. Something he was calling "Flue," and it was putting people down, sometimes for weeks. Bed rest and fluids were the only things he could prescribe. Loss of life would take a few of them, but most pulled through. He was at a loss as to what was causing the sickness. He was also dealing with the infections getting into some of the massive injuries, and his Cillian ointment was not helping. He needed new drugs for new conditions. He called on Bill Strauss for help.

Bill had been working on the infection problems since his animals contracted hoof rot. The rain of the new Planet brought mud everywhere and mixed with the animal's feces, breeding infection to the point of the animals lying down for days, causing stomach bloat and death in some cases. It seemed his chemical trough wasn't enough to control it. Luckily, some of the herbs he had brought, coupled with the extract of the local foliage, helped manage the bacteria growth. The pastie substance was applied to the animal hoof's heel and then wrapped in large leaves taken from the surrounding area. It was successful after four days when the wrap finally fell off. Just in time for the butcher, Duane would comment.

Bill decided to construct a dry stable to house the infected, which added more duties in that manual feeding was required instead of letting them graze in the fields. He called it The Animal Hospital.

Bill knew his medical supplies would not last in his new world, so he took advantage of his holistic training. The Planet seemed similar to theirs, so he knew where to look for building blocks. The mold of organic growth was his start for internal infections. Fly Larvae as an exterior anti-infection tool for deep-rooted conditions that his concoctions couldn't reach. It seems the little critters loved to eat anything infectious. Bee honey has multiple uses: It accelerates external healing and is an anti-inflammatory supplement.

Bill's concoction to fight infections didn't go unwarranted by the doctor.

They worked together on a thick paste, mixed with fruit mold and honey to help hold it in place and allow for better absorption. Finding and harvesting honey bees was undesirable, but the need warranted the action. Bill somehow managed to convince workers to do the job. The food offering was the deciding factor for most harvesters. The added benefit of taste made it appealing.

This new medicine was added to the doctor's supply. He would find multiple uses for the paste. He wasn't sure if the fruit mold or the honey was the magical ingredient, but it worked well. When taken internally, he had witnessed the mold reaction on bacteria in his lab back home and thought he'd try it on wounds. Whatever ingredient it was, he kept the successful formula the same.

******

Lennard had taken on the job of the landscape. With the laser beams equipped on all the shuttles, they could cut into the hillside, creating flat areas for planting. This made for quick work. By the end of the 6th week, they had leveled enough area to plant the year's supply. They all got involved in the planting season when the weather cleared and warmed up.

GC supplied them with seeds of all their crop variations for consumption—fruit and vegetables. Wheat for bread, which didn't do so well at the higher altitude, so most of the wheat crops were used to feed Bill's animals. The rain was plentiful but caused havoc at times on the landscape. The steps started to collapse, making them sag downward more than was needed for proper drainage. The new project was to reinforce them with rocks around the edges of each step. The shuttles were relied on to locate and place the enormous stones to build the building support walls. As the weeks passed, the village in the mountains felt more like a home. Its location was secure.

Chapter 11

A Seance

Sarah Clark was settling in as the group's resident psychic reader while helping the Doctor occasionally when needed. With the reduced headcount, his services were less demanding than a whole crew on the Fortress. Aside from a few "on-the-job accidents," he was free to pursue other interests, and Jason Miller always had a project.

A new home called for new aptitudes. As it turned out, most executive professionals were forced to put their skills on hold. Everyone needed to pitch in if the new land was to be cultivated.

By now, almost everyone had heard of Sarah Clark and her clairvoyant abilities. They mostly wanted her to locate the lost ones from the evacuation. She knew this would be a subject that would surface and need attention. She had to be careful with her readings to avoid outright lies or misleading. She'd keep her diagnosis to common generic scenarios if she saw no hope. Although some were desperate, a restitution of souls was not always possible. This is why she never insisted on barter. She would sometimes accept services rendered like a skilled masseur. She would have them leave her a promissory note to remind them. A service for a service. She loved massages.

She was starting to accumulate quite an extensive array of costume jewelry and family souvenirs in the form of statues and bowls salvaged from the different crash sites. She often returned the belongings to the givers weeks later. Sarah saw it as they needed to show gratitude, so she temporarily accepted it.

The Mission

She and Bill Strouse had reconnected and were casually spending time together. Nowadays, having a confidant was comforting, and being such close neighbors, it made sense for them to reconcile. Some of the other mountain survivors were also starting to pair up.

******

One early morning, Peter visited Sarah, hoping she could help him locate his wife, Lisa. Although channeling wasn't her specialty, she agreed.

"I've been getting a lot of that lately." She commented.

It had been a year, and he had lost any hope of finding her alive.

In the commotion of that disastrous day of the attack, members were lucky to have barely escaped the ship, so Peter did not have a single object belonging to Lisa. Locating her might be challenging, he was told. They settled down in a traditional room of dim-lit candelas and soft surroundings.

Sitting across from each other, they held hands. Sarah closed her eyes and chanted. *Lisa? Peter is here with me tonight. He has something he needs to tell you.* Peter started to speak but was quickly hushed.

Lisa Sullivan, are you able to come to me tonight? Peter sat silently for a while. Sarah softly chanted something from the old world that he couldn't understand. The tension was so thick one could feel it in the air. He kept squeezing her hand until she moaned from pain. Suddenly, a gust of wind passed through her hut. *"Lisa? Is that you?"*

Peter gripped Sarah's hand tighter.

"Peter, please relax. You're not helping." Saraha said.

Eventually, Peter started catching on to the phrases of the chant, and he joined in.

They sat for what seemed to be an hour, then suddenly Sarah took a deep breath and held it in. Peter then heard.

"She will come to you, be patient, and you will see her again."

A voice came to Peter that sounded like an echo, and Sarah quickly exhaled. Her eyes opened, and she looked directly at Peter as if she had just woke from a dream.

After a moment, she gathered her composure.

"Did she come in?" Sarah asked as if she was unaware of the event that had just raised the hair on Peter's neck.

Both sitting in silence for a brief moment, staring at each other, Peter spoke.

"I think you may have channeled someone else."

"What do you mean?" Sarah replied.

"The words were coming from a different entity."

"Words?" She asked.

"Sarah, I think you may have connected with God."

She turned a little pale, and her eyes glassed over.

"Are you Okay?" Peter asked.

The thought of God actually being in their presence was a bit overwhelming.

"I have never done that before," Sarah said. "Your connection with God must have brought him to us. Did he confide in you?"

"He told me Lisa would come to me, be patient, and I will see her again. But it didn't sound like a man's or a woman's voice. It was strange. I didn't hear it with my ears, but I still heard it. I was looking right at you, Sarah, and your lips weren't moving."

Not remembering the events herself, a chill ran across Sarah to think God was so close to them tonight and that she had just been the vessel for that spiritual connection.

"Thank you so much, Sarah."

"Don't thank me; you brought us closer to God. I believe you are the parallel for God to reach us." She leaned in to embrace him.

"Prayers will go out," Peter said." "I came here hoping to talk to Lisa, but you gave me a different hope."

"I can only speak with the dead Peter. If God gave you that message, I'm sure she's alive."

"It could mean I'd see her in the afterworld."

"Yes, but I strongly feel that she is still with us. See if you can find something of hers for next time. A ring would be perfect."

"I have something she gave me for my last birthday?" Peter said.

"Good, it might have her sentimental value attached to it. Bring it in."

"Thanks, Sarah."

Personal items had been stored on the shuttles poised for the previously planned exit, but the explosion changed that. Luckily, on scouting, Peter spotted one of his bags on the desert floor near a crashed shuttle but nothing of Lisa's. Much of the interior of that ship was scattered about and gave the impression that it fell apart on impact and burned. There were no bodies.

"I should have been on that shuttle." He thought. "I'd be with my family."

The Mission

He was beginning to wonder if it all wasn't a dream. Had his family ever been with him? Why weren't they all together on the night of the evacuation? Was Sarah only patronizing him, knowing that HOPE was the only thing holding back insanity in times of extreme distress? He had questions. They had already lost some of the crew from suicide after the crash, and he blamed himself for not seeing the signs during his weekly meeting. Depression was expected within the group. Some were worse than others. So many hopes and dreams of the Mission had been taken away. Family's left behind.

******

Sarah hadn't come through to Peter in a way he had hoped.

If she was gone, he could move one. If she was still alive, he had to find her. He wanted his family back. If alive, they could be hurting. It had been so long since he looked for her. He had given up on the idea that they were still alive months ago. He had moved on and accepted the guilt that came with it. Peter knew it was unhealthy to grieve for long periods, but his longing was not ending. His lifelong dream of being the first to find and inhabit a new world and contribute to his species' perseverance was gone. He now, out of desperate default, focused only on the survival of the small village.

What he wanted to hear was that his family was with God. He needed closure.

He needed Lisa to tell him from the spirit world that they were happy where they were. The possibility of her being alive brought him anxiety. If there was a chance that she needed him, he had to be there. There was no question about it. The two of them were soul mates, and his children were God-given. "*Why have you taken them away?*" He would often ask in prayer.

"Thanks again, Sarah. What do I owe you."

"Nothing, of course. You can bring me a barter blanket if you'd like."

"You mean those GC-issued ones?"

"I know they're not much to look at, but they keep you warm," Sarah said.

He shuttered to think that Lisa and the kids might be in trouble and that he couldn't help. The months of scouring the land looking for a needle in a haystack had not paid off, and he now felt guilty for giving up the hunt too soon. He had finally busied himself to help soften his agony. Now, the urgency for finding them was returning.

That night, he couldn't sleep. His mind raced with dreadful scenarios.

"Tomorrow, I will meditate and pray for answers." He needed more information, and the channeled cryptic words were not enough. He wanted to speak with God himself.

******

The next day, after the seance, he started jogging around the village, consumed with thought. Peter sat down away from the people near a large shade tree to meditate. He chanted the words he'd learned from Sarah. Turning off his wandering mind and focusing on his breathing, he got to a state of total relaxation. He fought the slumber since the sleepless night was trying to step in. Dreams can sometimes be mistaken for messages, and he wanted to be awake for this. The day was warm, and the gentle wind helped relax him. Being far enough away from town, he still thought he could hear voices. They were not distant voices but still inaudible. His meditative state went deeper when he listened to the music behind the voices. Then, loud and clear came his name. "*Peter*". He focused on the music surrounding the inaudible voices. Then it came again, saying, "*She is strong with a noble destiny.*"

The words were so clear they immediately pulled him back from his meditation.

He had practiced meditation many times before, but it was never like this. It put his mind at ease for the first time in quite a while. He knew what he needed now. His destiny was to leave his pitty behind and help others. God was in control. In the end, Love was the word, and he needed to share that word with as many as possible.

Chapter 12

MEETING THE GOD'S

Janie was admired by her town folk for her independent nature. And yet shunned for her inquisitive mannerisms. When she wanted attention, she gained it. When she believed in something, she defended it.

She didn't believe the stories about a new war weapon landing in the mountains. Rather than argue over it, she decided to investigate herself. There was always smoke from a particular area, and she wanted to know why. She wasn't the kind to wait for the King's messengers to relay information. That sometimes took months.

It was going to be a long climb up the mountain. Janie knew it, but that didn't scare her. She was very athletic, competing in several activities women were allowed to participate in. A foot race was her favorite. She seldom lost, with her long legs and gainful stride. Medium size and built very well. Attractive and healthy.

She never felt like she belonged to the higher class and often spoke words about the Upper-Elite, as she called them, which would often backfire on her. However, Janie gained respect from her constituents by standing her ground when accused of breaking social norms. She couldn't understand how anyone could lavish themselves on riches and belittle the less fortunate... She envied her sister's ability to bear children but loved her freedom without them. She had chosen the non-domestic lifestyle. It seemed to suit her well most of the time. Often enough, she would venture out on excursions during the day. Hiking the foothills was a favorite of hers.

After loading a donkey in preparation for her journey, she snuck out of town just before daybreak. It was a full day's ride to the bottom of the mountain, and she was exhausted when she arrived. She found a large rock to set up camp by. Desert plains were known to get cold at night, so she prepared a fire to burn through till morning. She hadn't seen any travelers or army along the way, which was a concern. The fewer people know about what I'm doing, the better, she thought. The crackling of the fire soothers her thoughts to lull her off to a deep slumber. In the morning, she would start up the mountain.

******

Warmer days were starting to return to the Mission site. Everyone was busy planting the crops. One early morning, while spreading seeds, one of the farmers noticed a slight motion in the distance. Behind a bush, there seemed to be a wounded animal peeking around and watching the activity. *"Nothing alarming,"* he thought since they weren't to the level of hunting local game yet. *"Who's to say it would have been editable? I'll leave that decision up to the Dr."*

Dr. Strauss was providing for them well. He appointed a "Life Support" team to evaluate the Planet's food content. Bill's animals were doing well in the new Planet's environment, and some had grown almost to the size of their ancestors.

His team had found some small two-legged animals with feathers that frequently left eggs behind, which proved to be a good source for consumption. The feathered friends were also being considered a possible delicacy.

Later that evening, in the mess hall, one of the first public buildings erected in the new village, the farmer started talking about a field sighting he saw. Someone sarcastically said, "It would be best if you had walked over and checked it out."

"Not me," he interjected. "I'm just the farmer boy. Besides, it could have been hostile, and I wasn't carrying a weapon."

"To you, everything is hostile! Someone said."

"You can't be too careful." He replied.

"You should at least tell Paul about it."

"I will, right after dinner."

The Mission

******

A young lady, exhausted and injured, stumbled into the mountain camp on an early chilly morning. Sarah discovered her as she hurried along, carrying her daily water supply to her cabin. It looked as if the girl had collapsed since she found her lying awkwardly. Assuming, from the looks of her clothing she looked like a local inhabitant of the Planet, Sarah immediately helped her inside.

The woman looked tattered and worn. "She couldn't have walked here," Sarah thought. The terrain around their mountain camp was rough and treacherous. A few men had attempted it and barely made it back with injuries. "Not something a woman wouldn't want to do," she thought.

"Can you speak?"

Sarah asked as she brought the girl a cup of warm tea.

She said nothing, only gazing at Sarah's cabin's interior surroundings.

"You need rest," Sarah said. "I'll bring some blankets." Knowing she wouldn't understand.

Sarah had plenty of blankets she'd accumulated from bartering. She went to her makeshift storage unit and rummaged through, looking for big, thick ones she thought would warm her quickly. Hopefully, she wasn't sick, she thought. The Doctor will know. After the girl fell asleep quickly, Sarah hurried off the Miller hut.

Doctor Miller was cataloging his biotech roots collection in his lab. He hoped to make an anesthesia similar to the one back home. The patient's screaming got annoying while stitching their internal injuries back together. The injuries would sometimes be fatal, but until the local wildlife camp invasions stopped, they were left vulnerable. This was Zeager's top priority. His instructions were, "Never leave food outside, and to shoot on sight.

"Jayson? There's someone you need to see right away!" Sarah announced alarmingly, almost scaring the Doctor out of his concentration.

"Oh great!" he said. You're here. You will need to learn this new process I'm proposing. So, what's the emergency? What happened now?"

"I don't really know," Sarah replied. "It appears to be a local planet girl. She's pretty beaten up."

"A local what?"

"I believe she's from this Planet. I think she has navigated the mountain alone to get here."

"This I gotta see," exclaimed the Doctor. "Where is she?"

"I left her in at my hut."

"Let's hope she's still there. "

"I'm sure she will be. I don't think she'll get too far with her injuries."

"Let's go!" Jay replied and quickly grabbed his medical bag.

The villagers had all visited Sarah's place to see the native girl. The girl was tattered-looking but still a lovely woman.

"That ankle will take some time to heal." The Doctor said as he wrapped it up.

"We're calling her Mary," Sarah replied. "She speaks the native language."

"Well, Mary," the Doctor said, "Welcome to our makeshift home."

Janie turned to Sarah with a confused look, and Sarah instantly understood.

"You are amongst friends, she said. Please don't be afraid. We are the strangers here. This is your home." Saraha replied, touching her shoulder.

Janie then gestured with her palms up. Sarah took the gesture as a question.

"I'm afraid to disappoint you. We must seem like Gods to you. Now, sweetheart, you should get some rest?"

Janie then lightly touched her leg and flexed her eyebrows.

"It's a pain killer. It's a temporary fix. It will hurt again later, but we can help with that, too. It's a wound that will take time to heal. Get some sleep while you can. I'm sure the mountain took its toll on you." Sarah said, figuring Mary wouldn't understand.

"Gods?" She uttered.

"Not quite, sweetie, Sarah replied. "The Doctor gave you something to help you sleep. I'll check back in a few hours. You're safe here with us."

Sarah waited until the girl fell back asleep before leaving. She poked her head into the Doctor's door.

"One thing's for sure," Sarah said, "she worships the same deity as we do. Even refers to the same Name."

"Humm." The Doctor hummed, not knowing how to respond.

******

An entire season had passed since Mary came to the camp. It frustrated her that she remembered nothing past the meeting with the Godlike Sarah. Peter was spending time with her, teaching her their language and learning hers.

The Mission

Mary had changed the entire aura of the village. The crew quickly adapted to her persona and catered to her as if she were royalty herself.

Mary may not have known where she was, but she liked who she had become. Here, she was loved by all. With Peters's help, she caught on to some of the villager's language. As soon as she could walk with less pain, she started mingling, asking questions about who they were. The things she saw around her scared her, yet she still felt comfortable. The shuttles, the Doctor's medicine, all were a miracle. Sarah's cabin was conveniently located for easy access to the villagers, making civil activity easier.

"You are?" she would ask every new God she encountered. With limited skills, she would sometimes recognize the words spoken to her but always left them with a pleasant "Thank You."

Planets and the Universe were concepts she didn't understand, and she made a mental note to ask Peter.

The chariots that shaded the ground above her were building the village quickly. Carrying enormous stones into the camp, lifting them into place with ease. It all astonished her. Sarah had brought her some new clothes similar to the village attire. She thought she was slowly becoming a God. *Maybe she was meant to lose her memory for the transformation to begin.* Her God-like language skills improved through the months, giving her the luxury of cross-communications. This made life on the mountain much easier, especially when she could order her favorite meals. Peter would sometimes tease her that food was the better teacher.

******

As the day slowly winded down, the activity in the village was reduced to a few walkers out for the early evening stroll. As the day cooled, people came out and mingled with new ideas and new planet discoveries that most felt needed to be shared. Peter especially liked the chatter. It gave him reason in his life.

"Mary?" Peter peeked his head in the door.

"Yes," Mary replied.

"I wanted to come by and invite you to our condolence group."

"What is that?"

"It's a group of people in need. People that are still sad."

She looked at him as if he just said something threatening. Condolence was not a word she knew.

"Need to return home. Am I.... prisoner?"

"I don't believe so, but I don't make those decisions. Have you spoken to the Captain?"

"He take me home?"

"Maybe, where is home?"

"The Valley, I think."

"I was hoping you'd stay longer," Peter replied.

"My family, missing me." She said, almost as an automatic response.

"Do you remember your family?"

"I not alone. I know that."

"Oh," Peter replied. "I was kind of hoping you were."

"Need to find them,"

"We will, I promise. We think your amnesia will be temporary. It's already starting to return; be patient. It's not that bad here, is it?"

Sarah paused. She needed time to process Peter's words. He talked too fast for her at times.

"Would you like to go eat at the restaurant?" He said. "That's something we can talk about over dinner."

Sarah would regularly join Peter's sessions. The main topics were anger management, Frustration, venting, and accepting what God has planned for them. He hoped he was doing some good for his patriots. They all had everyday worries, and it was comforting to talk about it. It also helped Mary learn the language.

After the meeting, Mary and Peter chatted back to the dwellings. Peter liked Mary a lot. He didn't want to lose her but knew it was inevitable.

"See you at our next meeting?" He asked.

"Yes. I learned more tonight."

******

The following day, Peter knew the shuttles were going out to scout and thought it might be good to take Mary with them. It wasn't fair to hold her hostage even though that's not how it was. Maybe if she saw some of the landscape, it might spark her memory. As much as he didn't want her to remember, he also wanted to know more about her. Getting to know someone who doesn't know themselves was hard.

The Mission

He tapped the door frame before entering the room.

"Would you like to go in a shuttle with me today?" Peter asked.

"I am afraid." Mary quickly replied.

She had been wondering what it would be like. It fascinated her and, at the same time, frightened her to death. Although everything she'd been experiencing since her arrival on the mountain seemed scary, embracing their culture might help her overcome some of her fears.

"I need to put closure on the loss of my family. I believe that they crash-landed back when we first came here." Peter said

Mary agreed to a trip, provided they immediately returned if it bothered her.

"Of course. I have been out scouting several times with no luck. Giving up is hard, so I jump on board whenever they go out. Who knows, maybe one trip, I'll get lucky."

"Yes, Mary said. We will look together."

******

As the Pilot lifted off, Mary screamed. The feeling in her stomach made her a little queasy. After a while, She started feeling guilty, thinking, "*This can't be right. Flying was only meant for the Gods.*" She thought. Everything looked so small on the ground. So insignificant. Suddenly, they passed through a cloud, and Mary froze.

"What happened?" She cried, and the Pilot explained.

"No worries, it's just a cloud."

As a child, she used to sit and wonder what lived in those clouds.

Suddenly, the Pilot banked to the right to avoid birds. "Oh God!" she exclaimed, and Peter looked at her as she clung to his shoulders.

"Someday, we'll have to sit and talk about what God means to you."

As they flew over the landscape, trying to stay out of sight of the people on the ground, Peter explained the power glasses he used to scan the area. "There might be a new village or a holdout for a small group. We'd go in for a closer look if one was spotted."

He saw a crash site with many people around it, but it didn't seem consistent. It looked as if the natives were sifting through the wreckage.

"The locals have discovered one of our crash sites," Peter told the Pilot.

"Yeah, we've been monitoring that one for a while. Wreckage keeps getting taken away. There's a town about 25 miles from there. It must be their headquarters."

"Could we come back later, after the people have gone? I want to check for personal belongings."

"Usually, I'd say yes, but they haven't left the site. More people arrive each time we pass over. As you can see, they are camped out down there."

"Maybe I could walk in from a distance out. I might blend in," Peter said.

"I don't think so, Sir. There's nothing for miles around. You'd have difficulty convincing them you're just a nomad drifter."

"Well, Map mark it, could you. Maybe another time."

"Will do," the Pilot replied. Although, he'd been by the site enough to find it in the dark by now.

They flew for another hour, and just when Mary was starting to enjoy the view, the Pilot said

"We're gonna need replenishing. I'm heading in.

As they swung in low, just as the mountains started their climb, they saw a lonely man on a horse.

"Use glasses ?" Mary asked Peter.

"Sure."

She could make out a man's clothing as she focused on it. The hat looked vaguely familiar.

"Think I know him," she said.

"Possibly," Peter replied

The shuttle gently turned to reposition itself towards the camp. The change caused Mary to dive into Peter's arms. He held her until the shuttle touched down at camp.

Chapter 13

ALL THE KINGS MEN

King Philip Losar (aka Phi) was a curmudgeonly dog-looking man. Named King for his bloodline only. His gruff manner certainly did not fit his position. He dabbled with many interests. He attempted to compensate for his appearance by wearing shiny jewelry. He was constantly searching for new gemstones. Always something different, which created a contrasting look to an odd opposite portrayal. Depending on the circumstances, he could also be a kind and giving man. It wasn't that he was evil, just unpredictable. To call him moody would be an understatement.

He took advantage of his position and wasn't afraid to let it be known. He thought, *"The more his people knew about him, the more respect they will have."* He was generous and always saw that his faithful were well cared for. He provided a clean city environment that gave the people security. His army was top-notch, thanks to his trusted Generals. He knew he would have enough followers to defend his reign if an outside threat occurred because the city considered the Palace sacred. It brought them prosperity in the laws enforced by the King's court. Without it, the city would fall.

The operational management of the court was responsible for maintaining adequate internal controls and executing risk procedures on a day-to-day basis. Identifying and assessing actions taken for mitigating combat edificate. The Palace was considered the first line of defense. It recruited soldiers, allocated weapons, and executed strategies.

Zackery was a senior court member of the organization. His participation was not daily, although the King would inform him of minor changes in his absence. He was always present during a judgment determination and new proposed strategies. He had no immediate family, so he was revered by the King. Zackery was always at the King's service.

******

Heliopolis was a growing metropolis filled with all the amenities and luxuries an oasis city should have. It was considered the most inhabitable, sought-after place to live. It held its popularity due to the simple fact that it had running water throughout. Beautiful single-family habitats of contemporary style dotted the hillside. The city had roads leading in different directions. Travelers could reach another small yet well-to-do sister city, also ruled by Phi Losar, for trade in less than a week with the relatively smooth terrain. With a town of this size, work was always available. The economy was more robust, so the wages were adjusted to compensate. The population grew with each season.

The King's military force was substantial in number. Young men were expected to join the King's service before becoming full-grown. They were not allowed to invest in property, women, and businesses until they had given 5 years of alliance to the country. After that, the King would assist in their acclimation into the world.

Phi Losar had reigned for most of his adult life. Accumulating his riches through heavy taxes applied to the workers. His reign encompassed an area of over one thousand square miles. His armies were loyal, according to Lozar, and in turn, his Generals were empowered to make all judgment calls regarding war. The King's only requirement was to receive a summary report of the maneuvering activities. Not being a fighting man himself, he allowed the armies to decide their own fate. Any significant decisions were made by the wide-bodied government, which consisted of high-ranking Generals.

******

General Zackery constantly traveled, marching his soldiers from town to town, persuading the people to join the King's ranks, and making offers they couldn't refuse. Sleeping on the ground seemed to comfort him over any bed. He

The Mission

was roused by a bright light filling the night sky. His army was settling down from a hard day's walk when suddenly Zackery saw the bright flash in the night sky.

Leo, second in command, had served Zac for many years. He stayed close to the General most of the time. Sleeping not far from him while in the field. He always tried to keep within hearing distance in case Zac summons him. Which he did often. That night, the fire rained on the land.

"Was it the Gods?" Someone asked.

"Have the Gods been angered from the sins of war?" another man was heard saying.

The guilt was never mentioned, although this night was an exception. What they had witnessed was horrifying. Never before had anything fallen from the sky. Soldiers heightened their awareness, and scenarios circulated amongst them.

Acts of war weren't considered a sin since they did help Heliopolis financially. Every victory brought more capital in from the town's overtake. Some enlisted men felt remorse after taking a town for their own profit, which left the unfortunate village folks no other option but to join the King's reign and pay his taxes.

Zakaria's army had recently taken control of a town just 2 days ago. Leaving a portion of his army behind to align their affairs and reflect the King's demands. He would reduce his headcount with each invasion. He would be forced to return home for reinforcements if the victory didn't yield recruits.

Some villages were happy to see them, deliberately handing them the key to their city. They couldn't fight the incoming troops as they had no army themselves, so they welcomed the King's men if only for more substantial representation. With this, the King's reign increased slowly. In some cases, all he had to do was arrive.

Zack's troops comprised 400 men from several villages under the King's rule. Mostly young, with about 10% older, wiser men used as consultants for their experience and knowledge in battle. Some of the young men called them (The Orchestraters)

******

"Sir," Leo quickly replied. "God is talking!" They had all seen streaks in the sky before, but this was different. A sudden flash lit up the entire landscape and then was gone just as suddenly. Similar to lightning, only no sound followed.

"Send a messenger to the King. I'm going to head the troops toward where the blast hit."

Most men were tired, but after their last victory, supplies were plentiful, weapons were fresh, and morale was high.

Pack it up, men. We're heading for the fire. Zack gave the order.

******

After a four-day march, the army came upon smoldering debris and set up camp. Objects were scattered for acres across the plains. The pieces were unidentifiable and had strange-looking symbols on them. Intricate pieces of metal looked like parts of a chariot, only much more significant. The men gathered around in confusion.

"It's a flying metal chariot!" One said.

"I've Never seen a metal chariot."

"Maybe to fly, it has to be metal."

"Men! We don't know that it is metal."Zack said.

"It came from the sky! It must have magical powers," another replied.

The biggest question was, where did it come from?

"Phi Losar needs to see this," Zack exclaimed.

"I wouldn't know where to begin trying to explain it."

"Soldier, grab a smaller piece of that material and load it on the wagon. Prepare to bring it back to Heliopolis. I'll write a statement of our location and my plans from here. Tell the King I'll keep him informed. Grab the freshest horse you can find."

It was a full two-day ride into town with a strong horse. Pulling a wagon added time.

Zack's plans were simple. The debris had been spread out for kilometers. He wanted to find the rider of this flying chariot. He followed the trail of debris.

As he progressed, the pieces got more massive. Some were as large as a homestead hut. He figured the pieces were thrown by momentum from the crash site. The mother load must be enormous.

******

When a dispatch entered the room, King Phi Losar was bathing in the royal bath.

"Your Majesty, I bring word from the distant outpost of a massive explosion in the sky. It lit the night sky. Balls of fire descended down to us."

The Mission

"Bring me my robe," he yelled as he stepped out of the oversized tub.
"Now, what's this about Balls of Fire?" The King exclaimed.
"Yes, your Majesty, they burned until they hit the ground."
All the brigades stationed in the planes could have seen it themselves. It was quite a spectacle. We've sent a scouting party in that direction. It should take a few days before we hear back.
"Interesting." The King replied. "Approximately where were these fireballs seen?" he asked.
"Two days ride from here, Sir. Zackery is marching towards the smoke. It looks as if it's in the foothills, Sir."
"Excellent, keep me informed. Set up transfer stations for information sent. Make it your top priority."
"Oh wait, send a message to Zackery. The court will eagerly await his findings."
"Yes, Sir!" he said, thumping his left chest with a closed fist."
Transfer stations were small camps that nurtured fresh horses that could run full out to the next station. A rider could return to the city in half the time it would take conventionally.

******

Almost every day, a wagon would roll into the city with more crash site pieces. The pieces intrigued the King. Some were curved, with an open beehive honeycomb pattern in the center. Even the King's royal court was baffled. As mysterious as these pieces were, Losar saw them as an asset.

The strength was incredible. An army sword would not even pierce it. Blacksmiths were unable to replicate its content. The metal was a mystery. *Some new military weapon*? He thought. The debris was piled onto the road in front of the royal castle.

The more information came in, the more the King understood that this destruction could only mean one thing. This was not a routine military exercise. The war was imminent, and waiting for repercussions would have been irresponsible. They prayed for a logical explanation of these findings but couldn't derive one. This needed to be scrutinized to the highest level.

******

Today, against his wishes, the King traveled to the little town called Avaris. Luckily, it had escaped the fallout and existed close enough to it, making it a perfect location to discuss military actions. Only these actions differed from the typical army combat strategies that usually took place during wartime. The King's honored Royal General called a meeting to discuss the actions needed for the Palace's security should a war be declared. The objects found in the desert were concerning. A war in the sky was a new phenomenon.

As the conference began, some were heard saying, "It's a new weapon of the North." Others were convinced it was fallen debris from a war in the heavens. The King relied on Zackery for all his military decisions. Zack was his "go-to man." Whenever asked about his military strategy, he would refer to Zackery before distributing executive orders.

Zack was not as confident as he wished this time since the subject matter was a total mystery. By the time the King's metalsmith arrived, some new metal had been formed into shields.

"It's part of a flying chariot !" Someone suggested.

"How could a chariot fly?" A soldier replied.

"Okay, so, What explains the lights of the sky?" Zack asked.

"I'll tell you what it is. It's a wake-up call." Someone said. "We need to open our eyes and ears. Be ready for anything. May it be an enemy or ally. We should be prepared with a strong defense. Draft as many as we can for combat. Start training now! It's a warning of coming things, and I don't think it's good."

"Assemble the strongest soldiers," the King ordered out to his Generals. "Sharpen their weapons. Drill them for all-out war. Then, get them outfitted for travel and send them to Zakaria. He'll need more men. There is strength in numbers. "Zac raised his arm to verify the King's order.

"Bolster our ammunition supply, men," Zack announced. Pointing to the armament specialist.

Shields, Arrows, and spears were being mass-produced. The new metal made an excellent shield, and sordes were formed from the shards that were found scattered. They found that the metal wasn't heavy enough for a catapult, assuming it would fall short of a target and lack the power to do any damage without the energy of its weight.

"Zackerly, take as many as you need, go north, out as far as it takes, and start asking questions. Be discrete and professional. Use proper diplomacy.

The Mission

If you get any questions you don't have answers to, say you are only a liaison and that the King has purposely kept you from any pertinent information to assist in being unbiased."

Samual, Go South and do the same. And by the way, if you run into the clueless ones? They don't need to be informed just yet. Feel the general conjecture. Whatever you do, don't let out any locations. It could generate confusion and political discontent.

The rest of you get to work on our defenses.

Chapter 14

NIGHTMARES

Mary lay peacefully in her room that night. Her mind raced from the high adrenalin of her first shuttle ride, ending with Peter holding her in his arms. Many nights, they talked and cried together. Speaking from the heart and soul, they seem to have known each other from a past life. "*How could that be?*" They both questioned. "*We are from different worlds,*" but she hadn't felt this comfortable being with a man for a long time. Peter was feeling it also, and they both gave in to intimacy naturally that night. Just before falling asleep, Peter whispered.

"I love you," and kissed her cheek.

She smiled and fell asleep with tears in her eyes. Her dreams were coming more frequently. Some are more vivid than others. She saw crowds of people and a prominent figure dressed in royal clothing standing over her as she lay in bed. Someone from her past was trying to communicate with her. She heard a voice. Janie? Where are you? Are you coming home? We miss you so much. The King's face was the only one she could make out. A voice from the darkness spoke,

"Janie, why did you leave me?" She couldn't answer. The fear ran through her. She couldn't move. In her mind, she could hear her voice screaming. "I'm here! I haven't left. Please believe me.

Another night, after the vivid dream, Mary woke with a picture of the man she saw on the ground from the shuttle. She knew him. "He's the one that wants me home. He's the one missing me. I must return, she thought."

The Mission

The thought of leaving Peter was horrible. Peter was such a comfort to her. The condolence meetings, intimate dinners, and the exploring trips they took together. How could she leave? She was already in love. Life in the camp was so wonderful. There were so many new things and so many helping hands. She knew she had a family here but also somewhere else. A family that she owed a responsibility to. One that also loved her. She held her pillow and cried.

******

"Mary! Mary!" Peter was shaking her from what appeared to be a nightmare.

Mary opened her eyes and held her face as she cried.

"Oh, Peter, It was horrible. Everyone was screaming at me to come home."

"Everyone?" Peter asked.

"I don't know. The only face I could see was Joseph."

"Who?"

"Oh my," she paused. "Joseph! My fiancé,' I remember now."

"You have a fiancé?" Peter exclaimed.

"Peter, I think I do. I remember now. I have a family, too. Joseph and I were engaged to be married, but I must have run away. Oh, Peter! She cried, Was our making love last night a sin?"

Peter paused from the shock of the news. His thoughts were racing with the idea of losing her. Could it have been just a dream? Not all dreams are omens. They don't have to play out in real life." He thought, only because it was what he wanted to believe. He knew it wasn't an omen. Her memory was returning; there was no denying that.

"God felt our attraction, Mary, saw our needs, and brought us together."

"I love you, Peter," Mary exclaimed. "I'm sure it was an arranged marriage and unwanted. Why else would I have run away?"

"Perhaps you will remember that as well," Peter replied. "What God intends, we must abide, Mary. I will never leave you." And then immediately thought, *It wasn't fair to hold her like that. His need to fill the void of losing Lisa must have overpowered his empathy."* He knew he had to let her go.

Gary Robert Smith

******

Joseph sat quivering by his small campfire, trying to keep warm. The air had thinned around him, being higher in elevation and much colder. The faint trail he had been traveling for the last two days was almost nonexistent from lack of use. His motivation to find Janie had practically vanished.

She could not have gone this way; she surely would have perished if she had. This land is not fit for humanity. There is no point in killing myself to prove that. For all I know, he thought Janie could have returned and would be waiting for him at home. It would have been wise, and he knew Janie would have agreed, too.

From a distance, he could see smoke rising on the mountaintop, and for a moment, he considered giving it another try. Then, once again, a fiery chariot zipped by only much higher in the sky.

"I'm out of my world here. I've gone where I shouldn't have." He thought.

Running low on food, he kept an eye out for the small game. Exhausted as he was, It's logical to turn back," he thought. Janie was his reason for being there, but if the Gods didn't see it that way, he couldn't control that. He felt a God was telling him to return home as he traveled, retracing his route. His thoughts grew with anger. Why would Janie sneak away? Why was she such a curious girl? Her thirst for knowledge was a constant battle within their relationship. She never really fit in with the locals. She was always going against the grain regarding the village's affairs. Joseph often paraphrased for her, giving multiple excuses for her spontaneity. He was a bit older than Jenie and sometimes had issues with their age. To Joseph, her energy level surpassed his, often enough that he would let her go on what she called excursions.

The effort was so much easier going down. It grew warmer as he descended. There was a loud rumbling in the sky. Faint at first but grew louder very quickly. Joseph stopped to look around and saw nothing. The noise almost became defining as he covered his ears. He thought, "*More debris falling from the sky?*" It passed as quickly as it came, and he could barely distinguish what looked like fire in the distance.

"One of the Gods watching over him"?

He must have gotten too close and disturbed the tranquility of the heavens. Something wasn't right! He felt vulnerable in the mountains. He knew then that he had gone where he shouldn't have, and the Gods were angry.

Chapter 15

Captured

For most of the day, Raymond kept tabs on the short-wave radio. The continual static that annoyed him the most had stopped and got his attention. Focusing on the smoother airwaves, he thought he could hear voices coming through. His heart raced with anticipation. *"Had Poseidon finally found them?"* The home Planet seemed like a distant memory. *"Calm yourself, Ray."* He thought. He grabbed the mic and asked if he could be heard on the other end. HELLO, HELLO? CAN ANYONE HEAR ME! Ray shouted. The sounds were very faint. Ray could barely tell that they were even voices. He could slightly make out what sounded like laughter as he turned up the volume. "Hello? Can anyone hear me?" He said in a slower, more pronounced voice.

(AL– Oh,) the voice came back very slowly

"Hello, Hello, can you hear me?" He excitedly exclaimed

Again, slowly, *(al-Oh,)* the voice repeated

I've got to let the Captain know about this right away, he thought as he raced out of the room. As he ran through the street, he stopped by to alert Lenny.

"LENNY!" He shouted from the doorway, "Meet me in the radio room! ASAP!!"

As Raymond approached, the Captain crossed the street in front of the unfinished hospital building.

"Captain! I need to show you something!" Ray almost screaming

"Can it wait? I need to have Jason look at this wound on my shoulder. My sparring partner got a little carried away this morning."

"We have Radio contact, Sir!"

Leonard was already there when the Captain arrived. He was trying to communicate when the two men walked in.

"Are they still there?" Ray excitedly said

"Sir, I believe we have contacted another race. It's a language I don't understand." Lenny had fine-tuned the frequency to where the voices were clear enough to distinguish them. They keep repeating the phrase, (*al oh*) and then laughing. "I can hear a voice behind rambling very fast, but I can't make out the words," Lenny said.

"I'm sure this Planet would not be using radios. Much too primitive." The Captain commented. "I recognize the signal as being one of ours. I suspect the radio has been salvaged from one of our downed shuttles."

"Another species, ya think?" The Captain asked. "Possibly." Lenny replied, "Could be a space station somewhere. Our entry to this Planet was brief, to say the least. We didn't get too much time to look around. I think whoever brought us down here is at the other end of that frequency." Ray replied.

"Let's not assume the worst just yet. Go ahead and monitor the broadcast, but don't return any. Who do we have that is good with languages?"

"Mary may know it. She has her language. She didn't speak ours for the first three months she was with us." Ray replied.

******

"The Captain summoned Mary to the radio hut.

"I hear your memory is starting to return.

"Yes, completely, sir, thanks to Peter. He's been so supportive."

"We have been receiving radio signals but are unaware of who is at the other end. It's a language we are unfamiliar with. I'd like you to listen and see if you can identify it."

She moved in close to the receiver and sat motionless, listening intently, unsure what she was listening to. Radio was another one of the God people's miracles.

"Yes, I recognize these sounds. They are Pirates. I've heard that spoken in the fields. Very evil. They kill for sport." Mary said. "King Losar has fought them for years. They wander the plains, grabbing shepherds from their flock

The Mission

and leaving the animals wandering alone. Our hunters have captured some of the sheep and brought them back to us, but we've lost quite a few. They also steal children from the villages at night."

"They don't steal any sheep?" The Captain asked.

"It's said that they eat their own. They serve no purpose here on Earth," Mary replied.

"They are obviously much more than a slight menace." The Captain commented.

"Oh yes! Many in the villages have just disappeared."

"Mary," The Captain said. "We were brought down to your Planet abruptly. We were attacked by an unknown force. I'm now convinced it was the Pirates. It may be that they have confiscated our people as well. Do you know where they came from?"

"The Pirates were here before my time, Captain. I've never seen one up close. I remember the King telling us once that they were completely different from us, but no one believed they came from the heavens. I believe they came from the Earth's bowels, where evil resides. They put fear in the hearts of even the bravest warriors."

"Maybe we could help somehow. Although we don't have an army, we have weaponry."

"Oh, Captain! That would be great. With your knowledge, I'm sure you will win any fight."

"There is a problem with that proposal. We, here at our village, are weak in number."

Peter happened to walk in from one of his group meetings looking for Mary when he overheard most of the conversation. "Captain, if you don't mind me saying so, a merger with the natives could be the answer."

"I'm just ahead of you, Peter. If these Pirates are holding people captive, we must intervene." Paul continued talking to Mary.

"So how will we persuade the King to let us into his realm? He may not want any help from outsiders or an alien species." The Captain continued.

"On the contrary, Captain, I've heard King Losar say many times during his State of the Village speeches that the Pirates are unstoppable. He is always training his soldiers. There was talk that the King was considering recruiting us women into the fighting force."

"Do you know the King well?"

"I know him. I know he is aware of you only as a phenomenon. After seeing your ship crash, he has all his army's training for the Big War. I heard him say once that the world had a brand new enemy. To him, you're still a mystery." She said. "He doesn't know that he's preparing for the wrong war."

"You could be the one to set the stage, Mary."

She stopped and thought, " *He's absolutely right.* She knew she'd be a good candidate to represent a merger. A merger with an alien species the King hadn't met yet. "*How crazy that sounded.*" She thought. Her story would be one of the hardest to sell.

"Can you do this?" Paul asked.

"I think so. I could sell you as God's."

"Take Lenard." The Captain said, "Take this light with you if Len is not convincing enough. Offer it as a gift."

"A stick that lights up the dark." She thought. "That will be a good start."

******

Mary had become part of the mountain family by now. Earning the respect of everyone there. She was over her amnesia and back to being herself, a very headstrong, convincing woman. Mary wasn't sure what the word abruptly meant, but she felt it wasn't good. She was slowly catching on to God's culture, but so much had confused her. She later asked Peter about it, and he explained. "It means it happened too quickly to make any proper plans."

She also wasn't entirely sure if the name Captain was right. She heard Peter call him Paul, but everyone else called him Captain. She assumed it was a higher-ranking name, although Paul didn't seem high-ranking to her. He had a family personality.

******

Peter was apprehensive of Mary getting involved at this level. He was concerned that her returning home after a long absence might awaken even more memories that he selfishly wanted to keep silent.

"You will come back to me, won't you?" Peter said

"If I can't, then come for me."

"You can count on it!" Peter replied. "In a shuttle."

The Mission

******

"Remember? You'll be the brains. I'll be the Bronze." Lenny said while boarding the ship.

"Don't get involved," she said, thinking, *"Strong men can often cause chaos."*

"By all means," Lenny replied. "I'm just a speechless warrior."

"And don't worry about me," she would say, "I'm one of theirs, remember?"

"Of course," he replied. They had prepared to walk a distance to not be seen off-loading a flying bird. It was too soon to expose themselves. The clothes were of the local styles. Lenny's knowledge of her language was limited. She was planning to pass him off as a mute. The shuttle needed to land approximately two kilometers away from the city.

"We'll have to make this fast. The pilot said, "Be ready to jump when I say."

Lenny and Mary readied themself in the doorway. As soon as the pilot yelled, they jumped. The shuttle immediately launched upward into the sky and quickly disappeared. The jump twisted Len's ankle as he grazed off a smooth rock. This made walking into the city almost impossible. The further he walked, the more it hurt, and eventually, it swelled.

"Hopefully, it's just a sprain," Mary said.

"Maybe, can we rest for a while?"

The mishap had changed their plans. Len began to worry whether or not he'd be able to make the trip after all. They found a cave that seemed to be abandoned. Mary decided to go ahead from there.

"I'll bring a horse back for you," Mary said.

"I'll be fine. And so will you, I'm sure." Len replied.

"At least take my water!" She said and handed him the pouch. "I'll get more in the city."

"If you decide to come in, I'll leave you this note you can give the guards. They'll instruct you as to where I am."

She wrote in the native language, *Hello, my name is Len. I am mute. I want to find my sister Janie.*

"It might help if you are limping a little. It Poses less of a threat."

"I won't have to fake that. Good luck."

Inside the cave, it was more relaxed. The mid-day sun heated the ground and air above the desert plains, leaving it much cooler inside. Fragments of small animal bones lay scattered about the entrance. There were also indications of small fires. *"Possibly cooking?"* He thought. *Human existence: Looks like they've been gone a while.*

Sitting in a relaxed position, he eventually cleared his mind, slipping into a heavy meditative state. What seemed to Len to be only minutes later, he started hearing voices approaching. As the voices got closer, Len could hear animal hoofs hitting the ground.

"Al-Oh," Ray heard from the cave entrance.

The Pirates!! From the broadcast, Len thought. They're here!

Lenny wasn't prepared for a violent confrontation. His heart raced with fear. *"They must have a camp nearby,"* he thought. His curiosity got the best of him as he hobbled near the entrance.

Al-Oh? Again, as the voice came closer. Suddenly, they appeared. Backlit made it hard to see any definition, but to his surprise, they were much smaller than he imagined. Even smaller than the locals. He decided to come out into view.

The Pirates were startled as he stepped out with his hands in the air. There were several of them running backward. In the dim light, he could see their hand-carried weapons. They were similar to their own lasers, capable of cutting someone in half as quickly and efficiently as they could cut through solid rock. One of them started screaming at Len in a strange language and motioning for him to come out, shaking his weapon to show he meant business. Lenny tried to show them his swollen ankle, but they didn't understand. Or didn't care. The screaming got louder, and the insistence seemed more substantial when Len limped to the front. Being off his feet for a while had caused his ankle to swell even more.

This is not good, he thought. *They certainly have me at a disadvantage.*

They blindfolded him, threw him on the animal, and gave him the reins. *Thank God they understand that I'm lame and can't walk*. He thought.

******

As it turned out. The aliens had a primitive camp with mud huts for living and no comforts that Lenn could see. He was thrown into a hut with a single-window crossed over with steel bars. The daylight was starting to fade, and He was getting hungry. He hoped they planned on feeding their captives. He also hoped it was edible. It seemed the camp held a lot of prisoners. This was, obviously, a jail camp. If he could somehow get access to that radio he knew existed at some point, he might be able to alert his people. But as to

The Mission

where he was, that was a problem. Somewhere near the cave was all he had to go on. They were obviously warlike people. Probably focused on the personal gain from their captives. But I have nothing to give, he thought. The language barrier prevented communication.

Chapter 16

Your Majesty, Sir

"Sir, a young girl is requesting an audience."

"A young girl, you say? What kind of business does she possess?"

"She claims it is a matter of security, Sir. She has news of an external threat."

"Is she a warrior?" The King asked.

"Don't think so, Sir. She said it's related to the crash site in the field."

This got King Losar's attention. More news of the crash was always welcome.

"That's all I could get from her, Sir. She's asked to see you."

"Send this girl in." He ordered

******

As Mary knelt on the cold tile floor in front of the King's throne, she cautiously explained her association with the people on the Mountain. How she met them and how much they have done for her. The King listened intently for most of her story but got anxious when explaining why her newfound friends were on the Mountain.

"So, you are telling me these people are our allies?" The King interjected.

"They are peaceful and need our help defending against the Pirates that may want to harm them and our people as well?" She replied. Once she felt the ice was broken, she decided to open the discussion that would either make or break their alliance.

"Your Majesty, my friends have real magic to share, medicine, machines, and tools we have never seen before. They can help us if we will help them. They have comforts beyond our imagination. They can make severe pain go away very quickly. They can heal the sick. They can fly," she went on, getting a little anxious, which made Losar nervous.

"They don't want to harm us, your Majesty. They actually want to help us. If we work together, we can easily triumph." The King sat back with a look of concern. After hearing what Mary had told him, her story was so strange, it was almost believable. *"It would certainly help explain the findings at the crash site."* He thought. *"How could someone make up a story like that? That's putting your neck on the line. Does this woman have a death wish?"*

"Mary? Is it?"

"Yes, Your Majesty. I'm the one that went missing from the town below. I was meant to be Joseph's wife. My earth name is Jianie. My friends gave me Mary. I went out searching for supplies one morning and ended up lost near the edge of the Mountain. I saw smoke coming from the top and ventured up. I misjudged the distance, and I got injured during the climb. They rescued me at the end of my journey. They took me in and healed me. I was very sick, and they nurtured me back to life, although I didn't know how sick I was until I awoke in one of their huts. I collapsed in their entryway."

Losar sat motionless for a moment. Mary couldn't move from fear of his reprisal. Would he send her to the Gallos? Behead her and impale her remains in the town square, labeled as a witch? King Losar was not that vicious of a man. He didn't have many personal friends, making him more vulnerable to bizarre stories. Losar was clever, so Mary trusted his decisions and hoped his love for his country was genuine enough to heed her warnings.

"I have heard of you. You have been away for a long time. Were you not concerned about your family?" He asked.

"I'm sure they were worried. Your Majesty, I was very sick When I finally reached the city on the Mountain. I didn't know where I was or who I was. They called it amnesia. Told me it was a sickness of the mind. The good Doctor explained it to me. In times of extreme trauma, you can often shut down and remove your memory. The memory can, but not always, restore itself if fragments of your past spark it. It wasn't until I saw Josphe in the plains that I slowly returned portions of my memory.

She knew that Joseph was not in love with her, and she was not with him. He was merely a comfort to her, knowing he was there to protect her honor if anything else. She probably would never have left him if a real relationship existed between them. Joseph was a tender man who cared for her dearly, but between them, they lacked the chemistry it took to bond together. That was the main reason for prolonging the wedding plans. They just weren't sure. Mary thought of Peter waiting for her on the Mountain. He was holding her when her memory started returning. She realized at that moment what she had done. She had been promised to Joseph but had given her heart to Peter, and it hurt her to think of hurting either one.

"Have you been to see Joseph since your memory has returned?"

"No, He may reject me after this." Mary wiped her eyes and nose.

"Your Majesty, it has been a very emotional and painful year for me. I've lost some friends and made new friends. My life has changed entirely, and I've changed inside. I know you don't want to hear my complaints. You probably won't believe my stories, but I'm here to say difficult times are coming. The Pirates can, and likely will, create a world war. They are vital in the body and in weapons. I know my newfound friends are equally as strong but weak in number. So, I ask you. Can you, and will you, please help them help us. With their weapons, we will surely overpower the enemy. We'll stand a much better chance of winning.

"As you know, Pirates are stealthy, ruthless, and fast. They won't negotiate, and, certainly, they won't compromise." The King advised her. "Were your friends the cause of the crash site on the hill?" The King asked

"They didn't cause it; they were victims of it. They came from a fortress in the sky, which fell to the ground after being attacked by these filthy Pirates."

"Fortress! In the sky?" Losar shouted. "Do you realize how bizarre all this sounds?"

"I do, your Majesty. But how else do we explain the burning debris in the fields? I know it seems unbelievable, but I've been there. I've met them. They're so much further advanced and knowledgeable than we are."

The King stood and started to pace the room. With clenched fists, he almost shouted out.

"Pirates! They've been capturing and killing our locals for years. It's time it stopped." As he turned to his guards, he instructed them.

"Gather all counselors in the war room. We will need to discuss this further." He insisted.

"Yes, Sir," a Squire quickly replied as he hurried out of the room.

The Mission

"We are still analyzing the remains of that crash. Whoever they are, they are far above our metallurgical skills. I want to meet these friends of yours ."

"I can arrange a meeting at your convenience, your Majesty."

"I will let all my constituents know of this. They, too, shall need to be present at this meeting."

"Yes, your, Magisty," Janie bowed and stepped back. "Will five days be enough to gather your troops?"

"Better make it nine."

Phi Losar dismissed Janie and gave her a safe, escorted passage home. He turned to the guards and spoke. "This could either be a blessing or a damnation." He started out. "One thing is certain; she'll make it easy either way. She's bringing them to us, and If they are hostile, we'll be ready."

******

The war room was set with a large round table built for viewing all involved. They needed to see expressions. War should be taken seriously, and Losar thought it best that all engaged in discussions could speak face to face.

Wars were familiar to the King. He had managed to maintain it through several iterations for most of his reign. He didn't know that this time would be nothing like the wars he had experienced before.

******

The ride via horseback seemed much quicker than the walk she took the day before. Mary was worried about Lenny. The preparation and meeting with Losar had consumed her thoughts enough to set aside his dilemma until now. He should have only been an hour, maybe two, behind her. She brought the King's men to the cave where she left Lenard. The cave was empty when they arrived. The hoof prints at the entrance told her he was taken by a horseman, hopefully not against his will.

Suddenly, she heard a rumble from the rescue shuttle. "Now is an excellent time to let them know about the aliens. The flying ship caught the King's men in total awe. With gaping jaws, they froze in place.

She had signaled the ship in the sky with a handheld light she forgot to leave with the Losar. The King's escorts were shocked to see a light beam extending from her hand into the sky but not nearly as shocked to see a flying chariot up close. The shuttle circled around and softly landed on a flat sand area. "*I'm glad the pilots are good at what they do.*" She thought. The ramp slowly dropped, allowing the Pilot to exit right before them.

"Kind of close to town, aren't we?" the Pilot said as he walked down the ramp.

"It doesn't matter now. I explained our technology to the King. Whether or not he believed it was something else."

"They should after these two friends of yours get back." The Pilot remarked.

"The King was gracious enough to escort me back home."

He was an older Pilot who still wore his military flight jacket. A symbol of prestige that the younger Pilots were envious of. The military had stopped allocating jackets after their economy dropped out.

It was dusk when they lifted off. The escorts stood in amazement as they watched the ship rise independently and quickly jettison into the sky.

"The King will never believe us," one escort said.

"I'm thinking he might. This will clear a lot of things up."

***

"Hi Mary, where is Lenny?" The Pilot asked.

On the flight back, Mary explained the mishap Lenny had encountered.

"It Looked like he had been taken away by horsemen. There were hoof prints where he waited."

"Who was your pilot?" he asked.

"It's done now. We need to worry about Len. I'm sure the Pirates have him."

******

King Losar sent a message to all the troops with orders to return to the city. His army's was evenly split up into 4 sections. North, South, East, and West were all at a maximum circumference of 50 kilometers from the city. It was a five-day ride, and he understood that the men would trickle in slowly throughout the week. He had his royal horse readied for the journey to the coliseum across town. With several battalions all gathering in one place, they would need a vast arena. He did not call an all-hands meeting often, so he started planning early.

His session with Janie was intriguing. Not wanting to be skeptical, he was still at odds with the information she had left him. If Mary had deflected

The Mission

to the opposing side, he would be ready. In times of war, one could never be too cautious, so he set the meeting in the largest building he knew of. He counted on her story about her friends being a small group needing help. Even if they did possess superior weapons, Losar would vastly outnumber them.

Battles were always a challenge; victories were a joyous celebration. Although, this new battle, if Mary was right, would be like no other. There would be no convening between leaders. It would be a fight to the death.

Everyone had seen the fire in the night sky. If aliens hid in the hills and carried fire-spitting weapons, it was assumed they would have no good intentions. The new firepower Mary spoke of was an asset. They needed to join forces. It was enough to scare the King into submission if the firepower was real.

Mary knew that Interplanetary travel was too much for the King to grasp. She could have mentioned it but didn't completely understand it. So she left that part out. It couldn't get too technical since it would only serve to confuse and turn the King away. He had to see it for himself. She hoped she had achieved her goal. She knew that King Losar could be a stubborn man.

Despite the Kings (no talk order,) the word got out of an enemy invasion. The gossip of Mary's meeting with the King brought more fear and concern to older people in the city. When the battalions started arriving in the town, narratives circulated. That same week, peace rallies were held at synagogues and places of gatherings. The young formed groups on street corners, promoting victory before the fact. The young town folk boasted, "Never give up without a fight." Neighboring villages were also caught up in the narratives.

Losar employed a healthy number of recruits in his military, but he always welcomed volunteers offering to help protect their heritage. It was a privilege to serve the King, and the long-term perks that came with it were good. The King thought it best to involve the civilian motivators in the meeting with Mary's people. Losar was anxious to meet these friends of hers. Anxiety peaked as the enormous structure slowly filled with all the King's men.

Chapter 17

No Casualties

Lenny hadn't slept since his capture. The lack of communication was driving him crazy. These creatures had no patience for him or his language, beating him as if he deliberately chose to speak differently. They assumed that he was holding back private information of some sort. His head ached; his shoulder blade was excruciating. Indeed, it was broken, he thought. Interrogations were getting worse as time went on. How long had it been, he thought? Weeks? Months? When, in fact, it had only been days. Somehow, he had lost track during the devastating damage they inflicted on him.

During one of his escorted trips to interrogations, dragging the chains behind him as he shuffled along, he spotted the radio they were unsuccessfully using. Len recognized it as one of theirs. It must have been salvaged from one of their crashed shuttles. He knew the radio was his only hope if he was ever to be rescued.

The aliens were a different sort. Speaking an utterly foreign language meant to Lenny that they were probably from a place far away from here. They were, in Len's eyes, lazy and forgetful.

They were hard to distinguish, with odd facial features and matted hair covering most of their bodies. They certainly were not aesthetically pleasing to look at. The alien's clothes looked to Len to be handmade, from sheepskin or some other animal hide. With no respect for their captives, they would sometimes throw them the leftover food they chose

The Mission

not to eat. He thought they would slip up eventually, and he had to move swiftly when the time came. That was if they ever quit beating him.

Then, finally, on the third day, the beatings had stopped. He was allowed to sleep longer than usual and started feeling better. The swelling from his ankle had reduced. They either lost interest in him or decided it was useless to brutalize him any longer. It could have been because they needed him to heal to use him for labor.

Then, one night, as unexpectedly as his life had become since his capture, the opportunity to move around inside the camp became available. He noticed his restraints started loosening enough to slip out. The one that tied him that night happened to be too drunk to notice. As soon as the camp's commotion had stopped for the evening, he quietly made his way to the radio tent in the cover of darkness.

He had somewhat calculated his location. They were nestled tight into the side of a small mountain with a distinctive, sharp-looking peak. Close to the cave, which distance he figured from the travel time it took to bring him there. "*They should be able to locate that from the air*," He thought. He prayed that the radio battery was still good.

******

"A full day had passed, and Mary was getting anxious. She woke almost before sunrise and decided to peek into the radio hut. Anything new on Lenny?" She asked.

"We got a radio message from him late last night," Peter replied. "He gave us landmarks of where he figured he was. He said to come heavily armed. Said his captures were cruel and abusive. The Captain is putting together a small rescue unit as we speak. I volunteered."

"Do you think that it's wise to go there? She asked.

"We know nothing about them."

"Just that they are armed and dangerous. I must assist in the rescue if there's any chance Lenn is still alive."

"I shouldn't have left him where I did. It's my fault he was captured. He sprained his ankle when we jumped from the shuttle. He told me to go on. He wanted to rest for a while. He seemed in great pain when I left him, but he wouldn't admit it, insisting that I go on ahead of him. He wanted a little time to rest. We found a small cave to relax in, so I thought he'd be fine."

"He's OK, Mary. We'll get him back. He said it was close to the cave."
"I wanna go with you, Peter. I feel responsible. I had just left Lenny there."
"Did you talk to the King?" Peter changed the subject.
"Yes, I did." He told me I needed to go with you on the rescue."
Peter chuckled at her sarcastic desperation.
"Oh wait!" She said, suddenly remembering. "The Captain wants me to attend his informant meeting." Peter pulled her forward and hugged her, holding her for a while. First things first, he said.

******

The Captain was explaining to the fully occupied room as Mary entered. "Mary! You're just in time. Come, let us know about your meeting with the King. As you have probably heard, Lenny has been captured by the same aliens we received on the radio five days ago. He contacted us on the radio; the Pirates had stolen from one of our crash sites. Lenny learned from his victim comrades that two significant pirate cities were occupied. We'll need more men if these so-called Pirates are all fighters. According to Len, these monsters are bloodthirsty. They have transportation vehicles. They also possess weapons, but he couldn't tell what type. We are preparing for the rescue mission to happen tonight. From what we could get from Lenny, was the building arrangement and geography. Seems all the captives are located in the long building in the center of the complex. We're going in guns blazing."

"The sooner, the better!" Someone shouted.

"And Mary, would you please inform the room of your conference with King Losar?" She had only confided with the Captain since her return

"Yes, Captain. The King will be meeting us in 9 days. I think he's open to my suggestions. He found my story so bazaar that he had to believe it. At least enough to investigate it."

"Not only are our people in jeopardy, but the King's people as well," Captain exclaimed.

"Pirates have been taking captives from them for years. Our pilots have seen some downed empty shuttles with no crash damage. We know now that they have a large portion of our crew captured. According to Lenny, the natives make up most of them."

"Sir!" Herman, second in command, interrupted. "The meeting must help convince the King of our sincere interest in helping them."

The Mission

"I agree!" Captain Paul replied.

"I suggest we land a shuttle in the Palace courtyard," Herman instructed. "He won't deny us then."

"Oh no!" Mary interrupted. "He's getting the coliseum ready for the conference. It dwarf's the Palace. Anytime King Phi Losar reserves the coliseum, it means he's serious. Killing pirates was at the top of his list."

"Well, we'll see what we can do," Captain remarked.

"I'll commission a few shuttles to rescue Lenny before they kill him. It's a satellite village and should be easy enough to take. According to Lenn, it has been hell there." Paul remarked. "I don't see any problems with resistance in the village as long as we move quickly. Hit them hard and fast before they can retaliate.

"We've already located the primary Pirate city. It is much larger than the village. We're betting that's where we'll find most of the other captives."

"Sir? Speaking of which," Mary spoke up. "The King is looking forward to a meeting. I didn't try to explain the space-traveling thing. I'm unsure if I understand it, but it might go without saying after he sees your flying shuttle. Be prepared for his astonishment, Sir.

Although I was pretty straight with him. In my youth, I never knew that the Pirates had been here for so long. The King has known that for years. He's known of their escapades, he just hasn't had a way of getting them back without marching foot soldiers into the camp and letting the Pirates overpower them in their courtyard. According to our King, the Pirates have superior weapons. The main reason they have been so successful at apprehending people."

"Some of which are ours," Herman replied.

"Probably more than we realize." The Captain added.

King Losar is tired of the carnage." Mary added.

"I see it as putting closure to a lost dream." One of the men spoke up.

However, we justify it, we need to save our people. I can't imagine what they are going through. GC sold them a dream and told them it would be safe. I owe it to them to bring them to their new home.

Did you reassure the King of our abilities?"

"I did," Mary replied. "I assured him he'd have a much better chance of victory with our merger. I told him of your weaponry and how you could fight from the sky. I don't think I have ever seen the King perplexed, but there were times during our discussion. Have I overstep my liberties, Captain?"

"No, No, You told him the truth. That's all we can do. I understand his loss. We both have a grudge to settle. We lost a lot of good men. Valuable men vital to the success of our mission, which they abruptly put a stop to.

They didn't figure in any of us surviving after their assault, and I'm positive that God will see to it that karma prevails. I can't imagine Pirates being good for anything in the Universe. They are nothing short of a diabolical menace, Plus!" he paused for a second and then added,

"I was kind of partial to the Fortress. It deserved a more honorable demise than it got."

"Sir," Mary added, "I'd like to go on this first rescue mission for Lenny? Since my people were captured there, They'll need my communications. But not just that, I feel responsible for Lenny's capture. I left him vulnerable and alone. I should have been there with him."

"I hate to risk you, Mary, but your language skills will definitely come into play. You'll need to convince your own to move quickly. The shuttles would surely frighten them. Regardless of how strange it looked, I'm counting on any signs of rescue that would seem like a miracle to them, and they'd move without question." He added.

"If you think they'll fear the shuttles, wait until we lift off. We'll have a panic on our hands." One of the pilots said. "Just tell them not to worry, Mary. Tell them they're going home."

"I want to station some ground soldiers around to help cover while we load the ships," Herman added.

******

At dusk, the shuttles headed for the Pirate village. The first ship held Peter and Mary with seven volunteers. Behind them was Herman and the ground crew. His shuttle circled lightly and touched just outside the perimeter fencing. Once all were in place, the seven exited the ship and scattered, placing themselves near the Pirate's barracks. Peter and Mary ran inside the long building, and with a mini flame thrower, they melted the locks off the doors. Only the new captives were still changed. Lenny saw the shuttles coming and had already informed the captives of the process. "Run as fast as you can to the big shiny ship." It was the only order he needed to give. The chained ones were hobbling, but surprisingly, they moved fast.

The Mission

The more activity outside, the more chatter, along with noise. Before long, the covert of the mission was removed. The Pirates, being understaffed and half drunk, were caught off guard. The ship was loaded and ready to go before any pirates left their bunks. The few that made it out started shooting at the departing ship but didn't hit anywhere that might hinder its operation. Herman's ground crew opened fire and laid down the others, running out before they could lift the weapons. It was a slick rescue. No casualties on Zeager's side. Herman got on the shuttle radio and contacted the Captain.

"Mission complete. Mission success. No casualties."

Chapter 18

A Grand Entrance

The shuttle hovered over the Coliseum. The majestic fountain was a marvelous sight approximately one hundred meters from the enormous entry archway. The area of the field was more than large enough to support the size of the ship. The people inside started to gather on the grounds. Fingers were pointing, eyes were staring, and some started yelling. The sight must have frightened some as they ran for cover. The King arrived and stood directly below, spreading his arms as if to say WELCOME! As the pilot slowly lowered his ship into the bowl-shaped arena, the natives scattered.

Mary had told him about the ships, but Losar had to see one to believe it. The description Mary's escorts had given him did not capture its presence. To stand by something so majestic was awe-inspiring, to say the least. The King couldn't believe his eyes. His heart raced with excitement. Some people stood still in silence, while others grasped each other in fear.

"The Gods have arrived," The King yelled over the hum of the excitement.

The shuttle's heat had warmed the area and took the chill of the evening away. The door dropped, and Paul Zeager walked down.

As he jumped from the cargo door, the Captain said, "Greetings to all of you. Is this a bad time?" Trying to break the ice, but then thought, "*What am I thinking? They wouldn't understand my words, let alone my sarcasm.*"

It was planned that Mary would help explain concepts to the King. Paul had learned some jesters and essential words of the locals through Mary, but not enough to converse.

The Mission

Thanks to Peter's tutoring, Mary had been in the Mountain village long enough to understand their ways and culture. Peter's support group taught her the language, and his love showed her the culture.

"Captain? The King wants to know, Is this your Fortress?" Mary said as they approached.

"You can consider it a Fortress, but no. We lost our Fortress to the Pirates. This is now our way of transportation," Paul said. "I understand your name is Phi Losar?" Paul said as he waited for Mary to translate. "My name is Paul Zeager."

"King Losar, yes." The King replied.

"King! Of course." Paul agreed. "Can I call you Phi?"

"I prefer Your Majesty," The King exclaimed.

"Your Majesty, it is."

Phi Losar was stunned to think that a God would look so casual. Paul had fashioned his wardrobe to mimic the local style.

The King motioned his squire to accompany the newly arrived party to the conference room. The space below the Colosseum floor was enough to gather both Paul's and the local groups. The beauty of the mosaic renditions of the King's family crest on the wall adjacent to the main entrance was so impressive that the Mountain clan shared the same astonishment as the natives had while entering.

The King loved celebrations and jumped at the chance to show off his wealth. He wasn't expecting this grand appearance but was glad he had prepared for the best. Mary's explanation of the honored guests was hardly equal to the reality. What he had painted in his mind did not do this justice. Feeling a little festive, the King led them to the meeting area where the festivities would occur.

Tables of food were laid out for the attendees to eat. Mostly finger food, with an occasional side plate of potatoes, prepared in several different ways. They thought the elegance almost mirrored GC's headquarters, but not the size. The Coliseum outclassed it by far. Eat! Enjoy! The King shouted. I hope our choice of nourishment does not offend you.

Mary, the Captain, and King Losar stood in the corner away from the dining and chatted a little to get to know each other. Paul inquired about the armies the King had. The naval ships he employed and the weapons he retrieved from the crash site. Captain Zeager called for Mary to help explain the situation regarding the Pirates. "We don't know how powerful they are." He was saying. Paul then turned to Mary and asked her what she has already told the King.

"I explained that the Pirates are equal enemies and that you want to help defend against them. Stop them from harvesting children and remove their leader. I told him the Pirates had captured your men as well."

The discussions went on into the night. By morning, both parties were on the same page. The weapons and flying shuttle were impressive. With Mary's translation, the Captain explained, as best as he could, the working of their fire weapons to the natives. He also needed time to train them in their use and accuracy. Air sickness was another concern. That could be remedied through persistence. Transporting the troops to the battle was essential in delivering soldiers with no marching fatigue and ready to fight. The Captain suggested that the men take daily shuttle trips and get used to the movement. Surprisingly enough, the majority took to it quickly.

The operation and tactics were different than that of the last rescue. It would be on a much larger scale. Both the King and Captain Zeager exchanged their experiences with the Pirates. Calculating the resistance and planning counter movements. The natives were trained well in hand-to-hand combat, but a hands-off approach was a new concept. Focusing more on the weaponry, Paul Zeager had a proven method of staging a field. The natives pushed back on many of his ideas but eventually gave in. Paul had left a world at war behind him, and his experiences gave him a unique combat education. He was hoping to avoid any losses but couldn't promise it. The strategy was one thing; bronze was another. The natives definitely had the bronze. It was his strategy he was counting on. He'd never actually fought a Pirate hand-to-hand before. He was relying on the King's men to come through there.

"I'll stick to what I know." He thought.

General Zachery was the toughest to convince. His arrogance was hard to break. It finally came to a compromise. Seems Zackery had proven strategies of his own, which was good as long as they stayed on the ground. Overhead fighting was a whole different thing. It came down to him commanding his troops and leaving the shuttles out of the equation. The Captain suspected Zack was more apprehensive about flying than staying with his proven strategies. Although there were many willing to fly and avoid the treacherous walk to the area. The Captain gave Zackery and his men a 5-day lead. The plan was that the shuttles, piloted by the most experienced, would be circling and firing while the King's men would advance and keep them occupied. The Pirates surely wouldn't be expecting a double hit. The rescue part of the plan was left open since there was no way to predict the resistance. With hope and determination, they would get them all out.

Chapter 19

The Final Mission

Every available shuttle was ready on the line. Peter had secured a position as assistant to the medical staff, including Sarah, Doctor Miller, and 7 trained helpers. With the damage the weapons were known to inflict, the earlier the injuries were treated, the better the chances of survival. Peter hadn't contributed much regarding the group's security in the past. He had occupied himself with personnel morale within his group meetings up until now. Not a fighter at heart, but a helper he was.

Mary gave invaluable service to her native people and the mountain people with her negotiations. The Captain had praised Mary for her help but held her back from this war. In Paul Zeager's mind, Mary was the holy savior. She was the one everyone respected and didn't want to risk her life. Peter wanted to help. "Besides," he reminded Mary, that the Med Unit was to remain above the fighting, out of harm's way, touching down only long enough to retrieve fallen soldiers.

The Pirates were indeed preparing. They saw the power of the mountain people and would be ready for them. Captain Paul Zeager knew this and raised the bar. The final war needed a victory before the Pirates retaliated from Zeager's assault on the satellite village weeks earlier. The timing of it was essential.

The King's men had planned to storm the buildings and clear out the captives. The King's army was in awe over the lasers their Gods had provided them. The new weapons were introduced to the ground crew and trained on their uses. Always stay alert. These new weapons are not a failsafe. The enemy will, more than likely, have something similar, if not superior to ours. Remember to replace your ammunition pack quickly. Never run without being loaded, and always be ready to shoot. Being able to point and pull was a new concept for the Earthlings. As the shuttles lifted off, Mary did what Peter had taught her. She prayed to a single God.

******

En route, the shuttles could see the Pirate's small camps scattered around the city. They possessed large canon-looking guns in the center of the complex. Tall buildings were built for lookouts with smaller buildings, they assumed, to house fighters and captives. There was a more minor sister village less than a mile away. Herman had planned to take that one out also.

The inhabitants appeared ready for war, as Herman suspected.

As Towers flew over the dark city, he saw the fortifying walls encompassing the entire complex. Their entry roads were fortified with what looked like more minor canons. The long, narrow building in the courtyard's center was suspected to be housed with munitions. Hermans's experience in combat was impeccable and given to him by the school of hard knocks. He informed his men as they started to go in.

"Just remember men, avoid targeting the long building in the center until we know all captives are out. Once that blows up, the whole place will go up with it."

Mr. Towers stayed above the fighting, assessing the situation from a bird's eye, helping to control the lower shuttle's strategic movements using the radio. He spoke in the mic as they descended into the hornet's nest.

"Watch your back fella's."

"That's your job," A lone Pilot replied.

They immediately removed the Pirate dilapidated shuttles, and luckily, they were all parked in a neat little row, making for an easy target.

"They must have known they would be no match to our ships." Herman thought.

The antique ships weren't a significant threat but were still operational.

The dilapidated condition proved to them that they had been here a while.

The Mission

******

Lisa Sullivan had not eaten for days. She had abandoned he will, since her children were both shot for insubordination. That's what the captives around her were telling her. The dark ones were unsympathetic to any of their captives. Most of them were beaten and starved just for being stubborn. Lisa had lost all hope. She was hoping that the aliens would come and kill her. She would scream at them when they'd bring the food. Pounding on the wall of her cell for hours, trying to upset the dark ones. She no longer had any reason to live. She didn't know if her husband even reached the planet's surface. The kids were with her when the Fortress alarm sounded. The idea was that they were enjoying the night shift's recreation center with fewer people attending, and Lisa had agreed to come along. Something she promised them she would someday do.

She always watched the sky in hopes of a mission shuttle flying overhead, but nothing ever came. *"Were they the only ones that survived the attack?"* She thought but quickly thought at the same time. *"If you can call this surviving."* She had been through hell at the dark camp. It had been so long she lost track of time. Picking up on most of the native language from the captives around her, she had almost forgotten her own. Hygiene was another forgotten past. She shuttered to think of how suddenly it all came about. How the dreams and aspirations of so many had been wasted. How she had lost her children. She awoke from a light nap that she had been doing since her arrival. It was her only sleep since she had not slept an entire night there. She suddenly rose up to a familiar sound overhead.

"Shuttles!" she almost screamed. A sudden warmth flowed back into her body as she jumped up and peered through the tiny window.

Nine shuttles circled the city in the middle of the night. The Pirates panicked as they ran from hut to hut while shooting at the ships, disabling the ones that took damage to their engines. It became a game to some pilots, avoiding, dodging, and dancing around the enemy fire. That's where the hot dog pilots came in handy. Two shuttles were shot down in the confusion. The more experienced pilots would circle low, creating a distraction by causing a dust screen, allowing them to load prisoners somewhat undercover.

Once they all loaded, they would pull back and open fire. Herman Tower stayed in the air while the others descended into the courtyard. The strategy was to have his ship away from the chaos below and target any potential threats from behind. Meant to give the foot soldiers time to remove the ones inside the buildings, marching the Pirates into the courtyard to be lined up to be shot. Afterward, the shuttles were to swoop up and destroy the entire city. That was the plan.

******

At first, she thought it was a dream since she had dreamed it many times before. Within seconds, the sound grew louder. The dust started flying, and laser troops stormed the gates.

Shouts in a foreign language filled the air. Before long, Lisa heard the voices she recognized. They were speaking the words she understood. A native soldier broke her cell door and shouted words she didn't understand. She followed his motion since he was obviously not the dark alien that had enslaved her. They ran into the hallway and into the courtyard.

Lisa immediately recognized the Mission shuttle and ran for it as it touched the ground. It was the medical crew's first landing, and Peter was helping the wounded inside. The minute she saw Peter, her heart stopped as she almost fainted from the shock. Peter turned to help her inside, and she moaned as if in pain, and he realized who it was. He froze when he saw her. Was she real? She had changed so much, almost sickly looking. He wasn't sure if he should touch her since touching seemed to hurt her.

Before he could decide, Lisa collapsed. The fighting raged as the fire grew. Both cities were ablaze and were obviously going down. They had fought for hours and had lost a substantial amount. The Pirates, admitting defeat, were starting to give up. The Medical ship was loaded completely. The Doctor had his hands full. Peter held Lisa in his arms in disbelief. He shook as he released all hope for his children. He at least had found his loving wife.

When it seemed like the war was ending, the Med shuttle rose up to fly off when a sudden blast of heavy weaponry along the road blasted it, spinning it in several directions. The crew tumbled inside the ship, rolling for what seemed like forever. As suddenly as the blast hit, the ship exploded, killing everyone on board.

From high above, Herman's viewpoint looked like a blazing inferno. He decided to swing down and retrieve the ground forces that had possibly not reached the retreating shuttles. As he neared, he saw the downed shuttles and the dead lying around. He recognized the men walking along the road, leaving the burning city. He swung around and targeted the ammunition house. It went up like an inferno. Assuming the area was clear, he flew ahead of the walkers and landed in their path.

The last ship and surviving soldiers were leaving the bloodiest, deadliest battle many had ever seen in their lifetime. Exhausted and confused, they seemed to have forgotten the convenience of the shuttles. The walkers were following their instincts and marching home as usual. They all eagerly climbed on board Hermans craft.

On the flight, Herman tried to assess the casualties suffered. He wouldn't try to guess the number until they were all safe at home. He finally landed on the pad just outside the King's Palace. The few men from the King's army staggered off the ship. Being more than willing to avoid the long, gruesome walk home, which would have taken weeks. They embraced Herman in gratitude. The King was waiting to greet the survivors with his Palace guards standing by his side.

******

A Victory, I assume? The King said as they marched off the ramp, the men from the King's army screamed.

"Yes, Sir. You won't have to worry about those aliens ever again. Sir, those are the same ones we have seen in the air above us. They are no longer a threat. We obliterated them, thanks to the Gods. We couldn't have won without their help. Bless them and thank them."

"Our infantry and missing townsfolk have been returned to us." The King slipped into speech mode whenever he felt inundated. "We have, indeed, been blessed. We've had a substantial loss and will Marter them all. They will be the ones to remember. The ultimate is we have met our God."

General Zackery chanted as he exited the ship. "Hail the Gods!" and the crowd all yelled at once.

Herman embraced the soldiers for volunteering. It was a great victory, and because of that, we all could live in peace. The Pirates were instrumental in forcing them to the planet, and karma finally came to be.

"*This was a great planet. Such beauty,*" Herman thought as he lifted off the Palace site. "*This is my home.*"

******

Mary waited by the landing area, hoping to see the Medical ship fly in. Maybe they stopped to pick up wounded and got detained, she thought. The day was starting to darken and come to an end. Mary returned to Peter's hut, hoping he'd be there. Maybe she had missed his returning ship. Herman had called ahead to the Captain to inform him of the medical ship's loss. Being shaken by the news, Captain Zeager knew he had to get to Mary soon. He intercepted her as she approached Peter's hut.

Mary! The Captain said as he approached. Let's sit, shall we?

He tried his best to soften the blow as he explained the dilemma. Peter was one of the kindest, most helpful people he knew. Paul reassured Mary that she had been a miracle in his life. She had sacrificed so much through her love for Peter and his love for her. Paul wanted to build a shrine in her name to honor the local people of this glorious planet. A building so grandeur that all who came to it will be amazed by its beauty. There will be a profound admiration for this shrine, Mary. We couldn't have won this war without your help and your people. We will build a Synagogue in your name, close to your city. You are a Queen in everyone's hearts. It will be known as Mother Mary's Mission. Paul knew his confession didn't help her despair at the time, but she'd at least have something to remember him by.

The Mission will be for all to come and worship as they choose. A house of God. A safe place of peace and happiness for all. We will build this for you and your people. She lay on the bed, trembling and crying. The first real love she had experienced in her life, and it wasn't meant to be. She remembered the first time she had come to the mountain. How strange and frightening it was for her. She remembered how sweet and loving Sarah had been. How she comforted her and treated the pain of her broken leg. How Peter made her feel so welcome there. How he helped her learn so much. Even taught her how to ask God for help in times of duress. It all seemed so surreal. She cried through the night, falling in and out of sleep. She lay wondering what was going to become of her now. She had lost loved ones before, but nothing like this. Her bonded, loving friend, Sarah, was gone. The good Doctor was gone, and her hopes and dreams were instantly removed. She had so much she wanted to say to Peter, and now it was not to be. The guilt she felt from the fact that Peter would never know their new baby was unbearable.

The Mission

******

She turned to face Paul. "Captain, I love you all, but I need to get away from here," she said

Paul Zeager summoned a shuttle to take her back to the little town where she had grown up.

Joseph understood her participation. He was not part of the King's army since he was too old to fight, although he would have if asked. His failure to find and rescue Janie initially left him humble anyway. It was not his place to dictate his beliefs and concerns to her. She was, and had always been, stubborn and set in her ways. Joseph was relieved she might still want to return home after it all. He was shaken when she suddenly appeared at his door.

"Joseph?" She said, "I'm sorry for leaving you." Expecting him to immediately reject her.

"Mary, they are calling you?"

"Yes, Joseph. That's the name they gave me."

"Are you here to stay?" Joseph asked.

"If you'll have me."

The End.

www.ingramcontent.com/pod-product-compliance
Lightning Source LLC
LaVergne TN
LVHW091600060526
838200LV00036B/929